"I have to warn y~~ou~~ wasting your time, ~~I~~ have no intention of being Christos Giatrakos's puppet."

"All I'm asking is that you listen to me while I convince you to come to the shareholders' meeting."

Sophie took Nicolo's silence as agreement. "Which bedroom should I sleep in?" she asked breezily. "As we are going to be housemates, maybe you could drop the Miss Ashdown and call me Sophie?"

"Housemates!" Nicolo's eyes glinted. "Don't push your luck—Sophie."

Dio, he had never met a woman so determined to have her own way! For some inexplicable reason Nicolo's eyes were drawn to Sophie Ashdown's mouth. Her lips were soft and moist and temptingly kissable, and he found himself imagining crushing her mouth beneath his own and kissing her until she was in no doubt that he was master of Chatsfield House.

Step into the opulent glory of the world's most elite hotel, where the clients are the impossibly rich and exceptionally famous.

Whether you're in America, Australia, Europe or Dubai, our doors will always be open....

Welcome to

The Chatsfield

Synonymous with style, sensation...and scandal!

For years, the children of Gene Chatsfield—global hotel entrepreneur—have shocked the world's media with their exploits. But no longer! When Gene appoints a new CEO, Christos Giatrakos, to bring his children into line, little does he know what he is starting.

Christos's first command scatters the Chatsfields to the farthest reaches of their international holdings—from Las Vegas to Monte Carlo, Sydney to San Francisco.... But will they rise to the challenge set by a man who hides dark secrets in his past?

Let the games begin!

Your room has been reserved, so check in to enjoy all the passion and scandal we have to offer.

Enter your reservation number:

00106875

at

www.TheChatsfield.com

The Chatsfield

Sheikh's Scandal Lucy Monroe

Playboy's Lesson Melanie Milburne

Socialite's Gamble Michelle Conder

Billionaire's Secret Chantelle Shaw

Tycoon's Temptation Trish Morey

Rival's Challenge Abby Green

Rebel's Bargain Annie West

Heiress's Defiance Lynn Raye Harris

Eight volumes to collect—you won't want to miss out!

Chantelle Shaw

Billionaire's Secret

HARLEQUIN PRESENTS®

Recycling programs for this product may not exist in your area.

ISBN-13: 978-0-373-13263-8

BILLIONAIRE'S SECRET

First North American Publication 2014

Special thanks and acknowledgment are given to Chantelle Shaw for her contribution to The Chatsfield series.

This edition published by arrangement with Harlequin Books S.A.

For questions and comments about the quality of this book, please contact us at CustomerService@Harlequin.com.

Printed in U.S.A.

All about the author...
Chantelle Shaw

CHANTELLE SHAW lives on the Kent coast, five minutes from the sea, and does much of her thinking about the characters in her books while walking on the beach. An avid reader from an early age, she found that school friends used to hide their books when she visited, but Chantelle would retreat into her own world, and still writes stories in her head all the time. Chantelle has been blissfully married to her own tall, dark and very patient hero for over twenty years and has six children. She began to read Harlequin® romance novels as a teenager, and throughout the years of being a stay-at-home mum to her brood, she found romance fiction helped her to stay sane! Her aim is to write books that provide an element of escapism, fun and of course romance for the countless women who juggle work and a home life and who need their precious moments of "me" time. She enjoys reading and writing about strong-willed, feisty women and even stronger-willed sexy heroes. Chantelle is at her happiest when writing. She is particularly inspired while cooking dinner, which unfortunately results in a lot of culinary disasters! She also loves gardening, taking her very badly behaved terrier for walks and eating chocolate (followed by more walking—at least the dog is slim!)

Chantelle is on Facebook and would love you to drop by and say hello.

Other titles by Chantelle Shaw available in ebook:

SECRETS OF A POWERFUL MAN *(The Bond of Brothers)*
HIS UNEXPECTED LEGACY *(The Bond of Brothers)*
CAPTIVE IN HIS CASTLE
AT DANTE'S SERVICE

For Adrian,

Thank you for 35 wonderful years together and for your support, encouragement and occasional tear-mopping through 25 books!

All my love, Chantelle

CHAPTER ONE

So much for modern technology, Sophie thought as she pulled over to the side of the road and switched off the engine. Despite following the satellite navigation system's directions she was hopelessly lost. The rolling landscape of the Chiltern Hills was spread out before her, but there was not a farmhouse or even a barn in sight, let alone an enormous stately home.

The country lane she had been sent down was so narrow that she shuddered to think what would happen if she met a vehicle travelling in the opposite direction. Sighing, she reached for the map on the seat beside her and climbed out of the car. At any other time she would have enjoyed the view of the English countryside in midsummer. The fields were lush and green beneath a cornflower-blue sky and the hedgerow on either side of the lane blazed with a colourful profusion of wildflowers. But Sophie was not on a sightseeing trip. Christos had sent her to Buckinghamshire to carry out a specific task and she was impatient to get on with it.

When she had set out from London two hours ago the weather had been beautiful. But now, although the sun was still shining, the air was strangely oppressive. Glancing over her shoulder, her heart sank when she saw ominous dark clouds on the horizon. Terrific! A storm was all she needed when she was stuck in the middle of nowhere. For a moment she thought the rumbling sound she could hear was thunder, but to her relief she saw a tractor trundling up the lane towards her.

'I'm looking for Chatsfield House,' she spoke to the tractor driver as he was about to turn into a field. 'I think I must have gone wrong somewhere.'

'Keep on going along the lane for another half mile or so and you'll come to Chatsfield, miss.'

'Along this track?' Sophie looked doubtfully at the road that disappeared into dense woodland.

'The road stops being a public highway from here and is privately owned by the Chatsfield family. But they don't bother to maintain it.' The man looked up at the darkening sky. 'There's rain on the way, and the potholes in the lane are deep. Be careful you don't get a tyre stuck down one, or you'll be stranded.'

'Thanks,' Sophie said drily as she slid back into the car.

The farmer gave her a curious look. 'You've got business up at the house, have you? Not many visitors go to Chatsfield. The family left a long time ago.'

'But Nicolo Chatsfield still lives there, doesn't he?'

'Aye, he moved back some years ago, but he's rarely seen in the village. My wife's sister works as a cleaner-up at the house and she says he spends all his time on his computer, doing some sort of financial stuff that has made him a fortune. It's a pity he doesn't spend a bit of his cash in the village pub. The King's Head is in danger of closing down because of this here recession.'

The man stared at Sophie. 'Don't expect a warm welcome from Nicolo. And mind his dog, it's the size of a bloody great wolf.'

Things were getting better and better! Sophie grimaced as she restarted the engine. She was tempted to turn the car around and drive straight back to London, but the idea of admitting failure to her boss was unacceptable.

Christos Giatrakos was the new CEO of the Chatsfield Hotel chain and had been appointed by the head of the family, Gene Chatsfield, to restore the once-famous brand name to its former glory. When Sophie had become Christos's personal assistant she had realised that the only way to deal with his formidable personality was to stand up to him and show him that he did not scare her. The rest of his staff might treat him with kid gloves, but not her. Few things scared Sophie. Facing her own mortality when she had been a teenager had given her a different perspective on life. She was proud that Christos had picked her from hundreds of other candidates who had applied for the position of his PA, and her pride refused to admit defeat.

The trees lining the track were so overgrown that they formed a dark tunnel, and the faint light filtering through the leaves cast eerie green shadows. Any second now she would find herself in Narnia! Impatient with her overactive imagination, she carried on along the lane and drew a sharp breath when she rounded a bend and Chatsfield House came into view.

Her first impression of the huge, rambling building was that it looked like a nineteenth-century mental asylum. Built of dull red-brick, the architecture was decidedly Gothic, and the leaded-light windows gave the appearance of bars across the glass. Even the purple wisteria growing around the front door failed to soften the house's grim facade. Sophie sensed that once it must have been a charming family home, but now the general air of neglect seemed intent on repelling any visitors.

Presumably that suited the only member of the Chatsfield family who lived here, she mused as she drove up the gravel driveway and passed an ornamental fountain that must have stopped working long ago. The pool had a couple of inches of muddy brown water at the bottom, and the stone statue of a water nymph had lost its head.

She recalled her conversation with Christos when she had arrived at the office at eight-thirty that morning. As usual, he had already been at his desk. He had ignored her breezy greeting and scowled when she placed a cup of coffee in front of him.

'Hell and damnation! Sometimes I am seriously tempted to dump every one of the Chatsfield offspring on a deserted island and leave them there to rot.'

'Ah.' Sophie had immediately understood. 'Which one of Gene's children has annoyed you today?'

'Nicolo,' Christos snapped.

'I take it he's still refusing to attend the shareholders' meeting in August?'

'He's as stubborn as…'

As you, Sophie was tempted to point out, but Christos's glowering expression made her bite back the comment.

'I've just spoken to him, and he informed me that he has no interest in the family's hotel chain or his stake in the business, and therefore sees no point in coming to the meeting. He then advised me not to waste his time or mine by calling again, and hung up.'

Sophie winced as Christos growled a curse. People did not hang up on Christos Giatrakos—not if they knew what was good for them.

'So what are you going to do?'

'There's only one thing for it,' Christos announced. 'I don't have time to deal with Nicolo, so you'll have to go to Chatsfield House and persuade him to come to London. I can't implement the changes needed to turn the Chatsfield brand name around without his agreement on certain matters. If he is as uninterested as he says, he might be willing to sell his shares, but I need him to be at the meeting.'

'What makes you think he'll listen to me?' Sophie argued. 'You've already told me he's lived as a recluse for years and avoids any kind of social contact.'

Christos ignored her protest. 'I don't care *how* you do it. Drag him by his ears if you have to. Just make sure you get Nicolo to the shareholders' meeting! Incidentally, I'll find it useful for you to be in Buckinghamshire. I want you to sort through some of the paperwork relating to a property owned by the Chatsfield estate in Italy. Gene worked from an office at the house in the early years and only started spending his time in London after the twins were born and his marriage to Liliana ran into problems.'

He smiled persuasively at Sophie. 'It'll be a nice break for you to get away from the city for a while and stay at an English country house. The grounds of the Chatsfield estate are extensive, and apparently there's even a swimming pool, which should be lovely to use at this time of year.'

Sophie looked doubtful. 'That's supposing Nicolo invites me to stay, which seems unlikely.'

'You don't need an invitation from him. He lives at the house, but he doesn't own it, and you have permission from Gene Chatsfield to stay as long as you like.'

Lucky me! Sophie thought now as she stared up at the imposing house. The huge front door was painted black and had an ugly brass knocker in the form of a ram's head hanging in the centre. Taking a deep breath, she struck the knocker against the door and waited for a couple of minutes before knocking again. Presumably Nicolo employed some staff to run a house of this size, and she was sure her loud knock must have been audible to whoever was inside.

A sudden gust of wind sent a pile of dead leaves scurrying across the drive, and at the same time a dark cloud swallowed up the sun and Sophie felt a little frisson of unease run down her spine.

Get a grip, she told herself impatiently. She peered through a window, but saw no signs of life inside the house. Damn it! *Where* was Nicolo Chatsfield? Christos had only spoken to him on the phone a few hours ago.

She had a perfectly legitimate excuse to drive back to London and tell Christos that she had been unable to find Nicolo, but giving up wasn't in Sophie's vocabulary. Ten years ago she had needed every ounce of determination and tenacity while she had fought for her life. Being diagnosed with an aggressive form of cancer when she was sixteen had been a shattering blow. One minute she had been a happy, carefree teenager, and the next she had been facing the very real possibility that she might die.

She had never forgotten the sickening lurch of terror in the pit of her stomach when the consultant had given her the news, the fearful expression on her mother's face. At that devastating moment Sophie had vowed to herself that if she survived her illness and the high doses of chemotherapy that were her only hope of a cure, she would live her life to the fullest, seize every opportunity and never be deterred by any problem, however insurmountable it might seem.

After everything she had been through, a solid door barring her entry to Chatsfield House was simply a minor inconvenience, she thought wryly.

Following a gravel path, she eventually came to the

back of the house and found a huge, overgrown garden. She imagined the lawn must once have been trimmed regularly, but now it had turned into a wild meadow, and the roses in the flower beds were being strangled by weeds.

The air of abandonment was tangible. She tried the back door and found it was unlocked, which suggested that Nicolo could not be far away. After a moment's hesitation she stepped into the kitchen and her attention was immediately drawn to the cast-iron range that looked as though it was an original feature.

'Hello, is anyone home?'

As she continued her exploration of the house her voice echoed hollowly around the wood-panelled hall. Various reception rooms led off the hall, all filled with exquisite antique furniture, including a grand piano in one of the rooms. She walked over to the piano and lifted the lid. Running her fingers over the smooth keys she was reminded of her father playing the piano at the house in Oxford where she had grown up.

She had loved to listen to him. They had been happy times, Sophie thought wistfully. Her early childhood had been idyllic, and as far as she knew her parents had shared a loving relationship. But her cancer had spread a dark cloud over all their lives and ultimately had destroyed their once-happy family. Her father's betrayal had been the hardest thing to cope with, even worse than her illness. He had abandoned Sophie when she had needed him most, and the hurt still lingered deep in her heart.

Abruptly she closed the piano lid and shut a mental door on painful memories. A sixth sense warned her that she was no longer alone seconds before she heard a low growl that caused the hairs on the back of her neck to prickle. She spun round and snatched a startled breath at the sight of the man and dog blocking the doorway. Both were big, dark and menacing—although on balance the dog looked slightly less terrifying than its master, Sophie decided.

The only photograph she had seen of Nicolo Chatsfield was an old press cutting from a decade ago that Christos kept on file. At the time the picture had been taken Nicolo had been a reprobate playboy who had seemed intent on blowing his sizeable trust fund on fast cars, vintage champagne and glamorous women. In his early twenties he had possessed the stunning looks of a male model from one of the glossy magazines where he often featured in the gossip columns. There had been no sign in the picture of the terrible scars he was reputed to have been left with after he had been burned in a fire.

Like his brothers and sisters, Nicolo's behaviour had attracted the sort of scandalous headlines that had helped ruin the Chatsfield brand name. But a few years ago he had suddenly dropped out of the media spotlight.

The man in front of Sophie bore little resemblance to the old photograph. His handsome features had hardened, and his slashing cheekbones and square jaw were as uncompromising as granite. He looked older than his thirty-two years and his unsmiling mouth spoke of a world-weary cynicism that was reflected in his curiously expressionless eyes. His thick, dark brown hair fell to his shoulders, and the black stubble shading of his jaw gave the impression of a man who did not give a damn what others thought of him.

Sophie swallowed. She was not afraid, but for a moment she felt overawed by Nicolo's formidable masculinity. He had not spoken and his silence was unnerving. With an effort she regained her composure and smiled at him.

'I expect you're wondering what I'm doing in your house?'

'I know what you're doing.' Despite the curtness of his tone, Nicolo's deep voice was laced with a sensual huskiness that sent a tingle down Sophie's spine. 'You're trespassing.'

'I'm not exactly.' Sophie took a step forward and hesitated when the dog gave a warning growl. She eyed the animal warily. She recognised the breed as an Irish wolfhound—with emphasis on the wolf side of its personality, she thought ruefully. The dog was so enormous that if it stood on its hind legs it would easily be taller than her five-foot-four frame. Deciding not to provide the hound with an early supper, she remained perfectly still as she spoke to Nicolo.

'Allow me to introduce myself. My name is Sophie Ashdown, and I am Christos Giatrakos's personal assistant. Christos sent me here to ask you—'

'I know what Christos wants,' Nicolo interrupted. 'My answer is the same as I told him on the phone earlier. You've had a wasted journey, Miss Ashdown. Shut the door on your way out.'

'Wait...' Sophie cried as he swung round and strode out of the room with his hound following faithfully at his heels. *'Mr Chatsfield...'* She hurried across the hallway after him but he took no notice of her as he walked into another room and shut the door firmly behind him.

'Well, of all the...' Sophie stared at the door and her temper simmered. She had never experienced such rudeness before and without pausing to consider her actions she grabbed the door handle and turned it.

Evidently this was Nicolo's study. As she crossed the threshold she glanced around the large high-ceilinged room where the walls were lined with bookshelves and filing cabinets. On the desk was an impressive computer system with eight monitors displaying constantly changing columns of figures and graph lines. She recalled Christos saying that Nicolo had built a career as a hugely successful financial trader. He owned a hedge fund company called Black Wolf Asset Management and was reputed to be one of the wealthiest men in the city.

He certainly did not appear to spend any of his fortune on clothes, Sophie thought, running her eyes over him. His long black waxed coat had seen better days, and his calf-length boots were scuffed. Curiously he wore a leather glove on his left hand only. If she had not recognised him from the newspaper photo she could easily have mistaken him for a gamekeeper, especially when he was accompanied by the hound from hell.

The dog was growling deep in its throat and the sound reverberated through Sophie's body. Nicolo was standing by the desk, studying the various computer monitors, and did not look round even though he must have heard her enter the room.

'Goodbye, Miss Ashdown,' he said in a soft voice that held a definite hint of danger.

Sophie's patience was wearing thin. 'Mr Chatsfield…'

The wolfhound bared its teeth. Nicolo continued to ignore her, and Sophie wondered if he would be even mildly interested if the dog ripped her to shreds in front of him.

This was ridiculous. She could not begin to persuade Nicolo to listen to her while she was staring literally into the jaws of a savage beast which had its hackles raised and its black eyes fixed hungrily on her. Sophie's only experience of dogs was her beloved Yorkshire terrier, Monty, who had been her childhood companion, but she was sure she had read somewhere that Irish wolfhounds were gentle giants with a friendly temperament.

The dog's gums were drawn back to reveal a worryingly sharp set of teeth. There was only one way to find out about its temperament. Steeling her nerve, Sophie walked across the room and held out her hand.

'Hello, boy! You're rather lovely, aren't you,' she said softly. She glanced at Nicolo's broad back. 'What's his name?'

Madonna! Nicolo cursed beneath his breath. Although he had grown up in England, he often reverted to Italian—the language his mother had spoken to him as a child—at times of heightened emotion or when he was annoyed by something. Right now, the something was the woman who'd had the audacity to stroll uninvited, not only into his home, but into the private sanctum of his study.

He dragged his eyes from the monitor showing the FTSE 100 Index and glanced over his shoulder, astonished to see Sophie Ashdown stroking the dog's head.

'Dorcha,' he muttered. 'In Irish it means *dark*.'

'Ah, I was right. He's an Irish wolfhound, isn't he?'

Nicolo grunted. In truth he was surprised by Sophie's fearlessness. Most people who met Dorcha tended to back away from the hound the size of a pony. With his shaggy black coat and strong neck and jaw, Dorcha looked menacing, but as he was now proving, he was a big softie who loved to be made a fuss of. Any minute now the dog would roll over and let the woman tickle his stomach, Nicolo thought disgustedly.

'He doesn't really look like a wolf,' Sophie commented.

'The Irish wolfhound's name originates from its use as a wolf hunter, not from its appearance. The breed was around in Roman times, and wolfhounds were used as guard dogs and for hunting wild boar and wolves.'

'Well, I'm glad he doesn't seem to want to hunt me.' Sophie gave a cheerful smile as she stroked the dog's rough coat, and Nicolo grudgingly had to admit that Christos Giatrakos's PA was very attractive.

He frowned at the thought of the Greek usurper who his father had placed at the helm of the Chatsfield Hotel empire. He had not met Christos Giatrakos and had no intention of doing so. For the past eight years Nicolo had distanced himself from the Chatsfield and had told himself he was not interested in what happened to it, but his father's decision to appoint an outsider as CEO had shown him that he *did* care about the family business.

It was more for his sister's sake than his own. Lucilla had worked at the Chatsfield's flagship London hotel for years, and she'd had every right to expect to take over from their father as head of the entire business empire. Understandably, Lucilla was angry and upset that she had been overlooked, and Nicolo felt a lot of sympathy for her. Hell, his older sister had done her best to hold the family together after their mother had abandoned them and their father had been busy sleeping with whichever chambermaid took his fancy. But instead of being given the top position she deserved in the company, Lucilla had been forced into second place and was expected to take orders from the new CEO.

Anger surged through Nicolo as he skimmed his eyes over Sophie Ashdown. How dare she walk in here from the enemy's camp and assume that she would be welcome? Every aspect of her appearance infuriated him: her chic linen suit that bore the hallmark superb tailoring of a top designer, her long legs in sheer hose and the elegant stiletto heels that made her slender calves look even shapelier.

Her hair was a warm honey-gold colour. He wondered

sardonically how many hours she spent in a hairstylist's chair to achieve the glossy layers that rippled halfway down her back. Miss Ashdown looked as primped and pretty as a pampered show cat, and no doubt she was used to getting her own way by fluttering her ridiculously long eyelashes. In his younger, wild days he would have been attracted to her subtle combination of sexy sophistication and he would have wasted no time trying to persuade her into his bed. The knowledge filled Nicolo with self-disgust. He despised the man he had once been, and he hated being reminded of his past.

'Dorcha—heel,' he commanded, and was gratified when the hound immediately padded over to him. At least he could prevent the dog from making a fool of himself over a beautiful woman. He glanced at the computer monitors. There was a buzz of activity on the Asian markets and the Nikkei was up three hundred points. He wanted to be alone so that he could focus on the one thing he was good at, which was making money, and he resented the presence of his uninvited guest.

'Perhaps you didn't understand me, Miss Ashdown,' he said as he strode across the room. 'I'm not interested in the shareholders' meeting, or in anything that your boss has to say.' He placed his hand on her shoulder and spun her round, feeling faintly amused when her eyes widened in shock as he marched her over to the door. 'Christos can go to hell for all I care. He has no right to be running the Chatsfield.'

'Your father gave him that right.'

'My father needs to see sense and put my sister in charge. Lucilla knows the business better than anyone, including Giatrakos.'

'I understand your loyalty to your sister…'

'You understand nothing,' Nicolo growled. The soft

expression in Sophie Ashdown's hazel eyes was the last straw. For a split second he had felt an inexplicable urge to admit that he believed his father had betrayed the family by handing power over to an outsider. Nicolo was not a man who shared personal confidences even with his few close friends and he could not understand why he had been tempted to reveal his thoughts to a woman he had never met before.

Standing close to her in the doorway, he could smell her perfume, and immediately recognised it as the Chatsfield signature scent. The notes of cedarwood, bergamot and white rose, with a hint of lavender, evoked mixed emotions in him, reminding him of his early childhood when he had visited various Chatsfield Hotels around the world with his parents. To this day every Chatsfield Hotel was subtly scented with the perfume, diffused through the air conditioning and also reflected in the range of toiletries provided for the guests.

They had been happy times, Nicolo recalled. His parents had seemed devoted to each other, and he had grown up in the security of a stable family unit. But then it had all fallen apart. His mother had walked out and he had not seen her again. He had felt devastated and abandoned, and when he had discovered the truth about his father he had felt disgusted.

The familiar scent of Sophie Ashdown's perfume mocked him. He did not want to think of the past, the things he had done, the regrets that ate away at his soul. He had found some measure of peace hidden away here with his computers and his work and he resented her intrusion of his privacy.

He steered her out of his study. 'You managed to find your way into the house so I'm sure you won't have a problem finding the way out again,' he said sardonically.

A deep rumble of thunder made the hundreds of small panes of glass in the original Victorian windows tremble.

'I'd get a move on if I were you, Miss Ashdown. The lane is prone to flooding when it rains and it's a long walk back to the village if you get stranded.'

CHAPTER TWO

For the second time in the space of ten minutes Sophie found herself on the wrong side of the door to Nicolo's study. Damn his stubbornness, she thought grimly, rubbing her shoulder where he had gripped her. She wouldn't be surprised if she had a bruise there.

Christos had warned her that Nicolo would be no pushover and she would have to use all her powers of persuasion to get him to agree to attend the shareholders' meeting. But so far she hadn't even managed to talk to him. However, she had glimpsed a chink in his armour when he had mentioned his sister. He clearly believed that Lucilla should be CEO of the Chatsfield. If she could somehow assure him that Christos was prepared to listen to some of Lucilla's suggestions for running the business, then perhaps he would agree to come to London for the all-important meeting.

The brief flare of emotion she had seen on Nicolo's granite-like features reinforced Sophie's determination not to give up. She just needed to try a different tack. If she went back into his study now she could guess what kind of reception she would get, but if she returned with a peace offering perhaps he would be more amenable and inclined to listen to her.

She walked back to the kitchen. It was lunchtime, and

it seemed like a good idea to tempt Nicolo with some sandwiches. But she quickly discovered that the contents of the fridge consisted of a lump of out-of-date cheese and a couple of raw steaks. Investigation of the kitchen cupboards proved just as unsuccessful. Sophie was desperate for a cup of tea but she had to make do with preparing coffee in a cafetière, and from the back of a cupboard she unearthed a packet of biscuits which she placed on a tray and carried back to the study.

There was no response when she tapped on the door. Undeterred, she walked in and smiled brightly as she placed the tray on the desk in front of Nicolo.

'I thought you might like some lunch but I couldn't make any sandwiches because you don't seem to have any food, apart from a couple of steaks in the fridge and half a dozen more in the freezer. I guess all that red meat is for Dorcha. What on earth do you eat for dinner?'

'Steak,' Nicolo growled, 'cooked rare.' His eyes narrowed on Sophie's face. 'What the hell do you think you're playing at, Miss Ashdown? I told you to leave— not scavenge around in my kitchen.'

'To be honest there wasn't much to scavenge. And it would have been nice if you had offered me a cup of tea after I'd had a long drive here.'

'It was your choice to come and not my problem that you had a wasted journey. I made my feelings about the goddamned shareholders' meeting clear to Giatrakos.'

Sophie had drawn up a chair beside the desk, but before she sat down she reached for the cafetière. 'I'll pour, shall I?' she said brightly.

'*Santa Madre!*' Nicolo exploded. 'What part of *get out of my house* do you not understand, Miss Ashdown?'

'I have no intention of leaving,' she told him calmly.

'In that case I am perfectly entitled to force you to

leave.' Nicolo jumped to his feet and strode around the desk, propelled by a surge of anger that surprised him with its intensity. For years he had stifled his emotions, determined that he would never again allow his temper to flare out of control. The scars covering one side of his body were a constant reminder of what he was capable of when he lost his temper, he thought grimly. *Dio!* But Sophie Ashdown had pushed him to his limit by barging into his home and disturbing his peace.

Sophie's heart sank as she stared up at Nicolo's furious face. His skin was drawn tight over his sharp cheekbones, and his eyes were no longer expressionless but were glinting with a warning that she was beginning to wish she had heeded. A purely feminine instinct noted that he had interesting eyes; the light brown irises were ringed with a distinctive band of olive-green and the unusual two-toned effect was strangely mesmerising.

She edged away from him and her spine came into sharp contact with the edge of the desk. It occurred to her that she should have told him she had his father's permission to be at Chatsfield House, but she had kept that trump card to herself in case there was an occasion when it might be useful. The occasion was now, she realised. But before she could speak, Nicolo seized hold of her waist and, ignoring her startled cry, lifted her off her feet and hoisted her over his shoulder.

'*Hey*—put me down….' The room swung dizzily in front of Sophie's eyes as he walked over to the door. She could feel her blood rushing to her head, but worse than the discomfort of her position was the loss of her dignity. She was outraged at being carried like a sack of potatoes.

'*How dare you!*' She curled her hand into a fist and thumped his back, but he took no notice and continued walking out of the study and across the hall to the kitchen.

Her handbag was on the worktop where she had left it. He picked it up. 'Are your car keys in here?'

'*Yes*. Put me down. I promise I'll leave.'

'You had your chance, Miss Ashdown.' His tone was uncompromising.

It was difficult to breathe properly with her stomach squashed against Nicolo's hard shoulder and Sophie could hear herself panting in time with his footsteps. She could not believe he was treating her like this. She kicked her legs wildly, hoping to force him to put her down, but he simply tightened his hold on her. His hand was splayed across her bottom to anchor her in place and she could feel the heat of his palm through her skirt.

To her shock, she felt a melting sensation between her thighs. She stiffened, horrified by the idea that she found Nicolo's caveman tactics exciting. She was a well-educated professional with a business degree and an executive secretary's diploma from the London Chamber of Commerce, she wanted to yell at him. He had no right to manhandle her!

He pulled open the front door and strode down the steps. The storm had broken and raindrops the size of coins pelted Sophie, quickly soaking through her blouse. She belatedly remembered that she had left her jacket in the kitchen, but even if Nicolo allowed her to run back for it, she could not contemplate going back into the house.

When he set her down on the driveway she was almost speechless with anger. Almost—but not quite.

'You—you *Neanderthal*! I've a good mind to report you for assault.' She clenched her jaw to stop her teeth from chattering as a combination of shock at Nicolo's actions and the sensation of being lashed by the increasingly heavy rain set in.

He folded his arms across his massive chest. 'You are trespassing on my property and I am entitled to use reasonable means to eject you,' he said coldly.

Sophie stared at his chiselled features and felt a dragging sensation deep in her pelvis. God, he was sexy! In his long black coat and boots he reminded her of a Regency rake from the historical romance novels she secretly enjoyed reading. She would never admit to the other members of the online book club she belonged to that she was a fan of so-called 'bodice-rippers,' or that she fantasized about being swept off her feet by a devilishly gorgeous hero.

She watched Nicolo sweep his long dark hair back from his brow and thought ruefully that a couple of centuries ago he was more likely to have been a highwayman. He certainly had a total disregard for rules and social niceties.

Christos would have to think of another way of persuading Nicolo to attend the shareholders' meeting because she refused to remain at Chatsfield House a minute longer. Her hand shook as she scrambled in her handbag for her keys and unlocked the car. She was drenched and her skirt clung to her legs, making it awkward for her to slide behind the wheel.

'Drive carefully,' Nicolo advised. 'Some of the sharp bends along the lane can be treacherous in the wet.'

She longed to slap the arrogant expression from his face, but there was a dangerous gleam in his eyes and her common sense prevailed.

'Go to hell,' she snapped as she slammed the door and started the engine. Seconds later the tyres spun on the wet gravel as she pressed the accelerator pedal and shot down the driveway. She glanced in the rear-view mirror, expecting to see Nicolo watching to make sure she left, but he was walking back into the house and did not look round.

Sophie drove as fast as the torrential rain and the terrible potholes in the lane allowed while she called Nicolo Chatsfield every rude word she could think of. She was still seething when she arrived in the village and pulled into the pub car park. But her anger was mixed with another emotion as she acknowledged the reality of the situation.

She had given up! Sophie Ashdown—who, as a teenager, had clung on to life with sheer determination, had been defeated.

She bit down on her lip. She hadn't cried since she was sixteen and had caught sight of her bald head in the mirror. At the time, she had lost her hair because of the chemotherapy and had usually worn a woolly hat that her grandmother had knitted her—partly to hide her baldness and partly because the cancer made her feel cold all the time. Seeing her shiny scalp that day, instead of a mane of long blonde hair, had forced her to confront the seriousness of her condition and the frightening possibility that she might die.

She had cried for hours, alone in the isolation room where she was receiving treatment. It had seemed so unfair; she had so much to live for, so many plans. At the end of the crying jag, she'd had a puffy face and red eyes to go with her lack of hair. To her mind she was the ugliest person on the planet, no longer the pretty teenager she had once been. Sophie Ashdown did not exist anymore.

It had been the lowest moment of her illness. But it had also been a turning point. As Sophie had stared at her reflection in the mirror she had vowed that she would not let cancer steal everything she loved. It had taken her hair and her eyelashes and her pride; it had taken two of the friends she had made at the cancer unit. But she had vowed that she would not give up her life without a fight. Having cancer had made her develop a steely determination never to let anything beat her. And ten years on, that trait was an intrinsic part of her nature.

Why had she let Nicolo Chatsfield get the better of her? Sophie now asked herself as she stared at the faded sign of the King's Head hanging over the entrance to the pub. She had played right into Nicolo's hands. His outrageous behaviour had resulted in her swift departure from Chatsfield House exactly as he had intended. Now she was faced with returning to Christos and admitting that she had failed the task he had set for her—or she could turn the car around and drive back along the lane full of potholes.

The prospect of facing Nicolo again made her heart lurch. The sensible thing to do would be to head back to London and let Christos deal with Nicolo. But her pride rejected the idea. Nicolo had won the first skirmish, but the battle was far from over! Determination surged through her. Somehow, she was going to make him listen to her. However, before she returned to Chatsfield House she would need to shop for groceries. She could handle Nicolo's bad temper, but the thought of eating the bloodied lumps of steak she had found in his fridge made her shudder.

Nicolo emerged from the copse at the edge of the Chatsfield estate and looked round for Dorcha, who was pawing at a rabbit hole.

'Come on, dog,' he called as he opened the garden gate

and strode across the wet lawn. After spending hours sitting in front of his computer it felt good to get outside and expend some energy. The storm had passed, leaving an overcast sky in its wake that belied the fact that it was midsummer, but the dank atmosphere suited Nicolo's grim mood.

Dorcha bounded ahead of him up the path to the kitchen door. The hound had been acting strangely all afternoon, pacing around the study and whining. Perhaps he had been unsettled by the presence of another person in the house. Nicolo frowned. Sophie Ashdown's visit had been an annoying distraction, and even after he had got rid of her he had found it difficult to concentrate, which had proved disastrous when he had needed to be completely focused on the financial trading markets. The result was that he had lost several hundred thousand pounds. The money was not a problem; it represented only a tiny fraction of his wealth, but he rarely made bad decisions and he hated losing a deal.

It was all the fault of Christos Giatrakos's goddamned PA, he thought irritably. The scent of Sophie's perfume still lingered in his study, which was another reason why he had decided to go out and get some fresh air. He could not understand why her image lingered in his mind. She was attractive, admittedly, but he was no longer the crass idiot of his youth who had been at the mercy of his hormones and had lost count of the number of women he had bedded. He did not want to be reminded of the person he had once been, whose stupid exploits had frequently made the headlines and whose love life had provided fodder for the paparazzi.

Dorcha was barking madly and jumping up against the kitchen window. Maybe the dog had seen a mouse. Nicolo pushed open the kitchen door and stopped dead.

'You, *again*!' he said harshly. 'For God's sake, Miss Ashdown, can't you take a hint? You're not welcome here.'

'Your dog is pleased to see me—aren't you, boy?' Sophie crooned as she made a fuss of Dorcha. 'Can you smell your dinner?' she asked the wolfhound. She glanced at Nicolo. 'I'm cooking a steak for him and stuffed baked trout for us. You really shouldn't eat too much red meat—it's bad for your digestive system and is probably the reason you're so grouchy.'

Nicolo's eyes narrowed. 'Is that so?' No way was he going to admit that the aroma of warm trout was tantalising his taste buds. Truthfully, he was sick of eating steak every night, but he had not realised it until now.

'I bought lots of fresh vegetables as well as store cupboard essentials,' Sophie continued brightly. 'The lady in the village shop said that you used to employ a cook, but since Mrs Pearson retired a couple of months ago you live here alone.'

'I *like* being on my own,' Nicolo said pointedly.

Sophie apparently did not hear him and prattled on. 'Although the shop lady said you have a cleaner come in twice a week. I knew that anyway. Your cleaner is the farmer's wife's sister, isn't she?'

'I haven't a goddamned clue who my cleaner is related to. How the hell do *you* know?' Nicolo strode across the kitchen. '*Dio*, do you ever stop talking, Miss Ashdown?' He swore beneath his breath. 'What do you want?'

'You know what I want. Christos asked me to talk to you—'

'Perhaps he hoped you would bore me to death.'

'—about the shareholders' meeting.' Sophie ignored his jibe. She turned her head and gave him a direct look that for some peculiar reason made Nicolo feel uncomfortable. 'I'm simply trying to do my job,' she said quietly.

Sophie stiffened as Nicolo strode towards her. 'If you're planning to use brute force to throw me out of the house again, I'd better warn you that I am perfectly capable of defending myself. It was just that you took me by surprise earlier.'

Nicolo skimmed his gaze over her petite frame. 'I'm a foot taller than you. What do you intend to do—bite my ankles?' he asked sardonically.

Sophie's hazel eyes flashed dangerously and she folded her arms across her chest. 'As a matter of fact, I'm a black belt in—in tae kwon do.'

It was true that she had never sparred with an opponent as physically imposing as Nicolo, but she wasn't going to admit that to him. 'I'll make a deal with you, Mr Chatsfield.'

'You're hardly in a position to make a deal, Miss Ashdown.'

Despite himself, Nicolo was intrigued by Sophie. When he'd walked into the kitchen he had been shocked to find that she had returned to the house after their previous encounter. She had guts, he acknowledged grudgingly.

Irritatingly, he was also forced to admit that *attractive* did not adequately describe her classical beauty. She had changed into jeans and a plain white T-shirt. There was nothing remarkable about her clothes but he could not help noticing how the denim moulded her pert bottom and the clingy cotton shirt revealed the upwards tilt of her breasts. Her long hair was caught up in a ponytail, with a few feathery strands framing her face, and the transformation from sophisticated secretary to a look that was both wholesome and yet sexy stirred a purely masculine response in Nicolo.

'What deal?' he growled.

Sophie felt a surge of triumph that she seemed to be getting somewhere with Nicolo but she was careful not to reveal her satisfaction in her voice. 'If you will allow me to stay and try to persuade you to attend the shareholders' meeting, I'll cook for you.' She smiled. 'Without wanting to boast, I'm a very good cook.'

Nicolo shrugged. 'I have to warn you that you'll be wasting your time, Miss Ashdown. I have no intention of being Christos Giatrakos's puppet.'

'All I'm asking is that you listen to me. Also, Christos wants me to stay for a few days and sort through some of the files that your father kept here.'

Sophie took Nicolo's silence as agreement. 'Which bedroom should I sleep in?' she asked breezily. 'As we are going to be housemates, maybe you could drop the Miss Ashdown and call me Sophie?'

'Housemates!' Nicolo's eyes glinted. 'Don't push your luck—Sophie.'

Dio, he had never met a woman so determined to have her own way! For some inexplicable reason Nicolo's eyes were drawn to Sophie Ashdown's mouth. Her lips were soft and moist and temptingly kissable and he found himself imagining crushing her mouth beneath his own and kissing her until she was in no doubt that *he* was master of Chatsfield House.

Madonna, that was not a path he wanted to go down, he reminded himself. He had no interest in Christos Giatrakos's ultra-confident, ultra-irritating personal assistant. He could physically evict her from the house again, but she would probably find a way of getting back in. She had proved herself to be surprisingly resourceful. His jaw tightened with irritation as he acknowledged that he would have to put up with her presence for a couple of days. Once she'd got the message that he would not change his mind about the shareholders' meeting she would presumably take herself back to London.

'You can use the room at the far end of the second-floor landing,' he told her abruptly. 'It has a good view of the Chiltern Hills from the window.'

'Thank you,' Sophie murmured. To her annoyance her voice sounded faintly breathless. She had noticed how Nicolo's gaze had lingered on her breasts, and she prayed he could not tell that her nipples had hardened beneath her bra. She was supremely aware of his potent masculinity and dismayed by the subtle undercurrent of sexual tension that she sensed between them. The last thing she wanted was to be attracted to Nicolo Chatsfield!

Feeling flustered, she swung away from him and walked over to the range cooker. 'If you need to carry on working in your study, I'll call you when dinner is ready.'

He muttered something beneath his breath that to Sophie's sharp sense of hearing sounded like 'bossy madam.' She could not tear her eyes from him as he shrugged off his leather coat, revealing a black silk shirt that moulded his muscular torso. He pulled the glove from his left hand and she gasped when she saw his discoloured skin. The scarring had the distinctive mottled appearance of a burn injury, covering his fingers and the back of his hand and disappearing beneath his shirt-sleeve. Sophie wondered how far up his arm the scar went.

Her eyes flew to his face. Nicolo had stiffened at her reaction and his expression was shuttered so that she had no idea what he was thinking.

'I couldn't help noticing your hand,' she said shakily.

'Christos told me that you were badly hurt in a fire years ago at the Chatsfield.'

When he made no response she continued, 'You saved someone's life. The papers said you were a hero.'

Nicolo gave a harsh laugh and his mouth twisted in an expression of bleak bitterness that shocked Sophie.

'You shouldn't believe everything you read in newspapers,' he said savagely. Spinning round, he strode out of the kitchen and across the hall to his study, closing the door behind him with a resounding slam that made Sophie wonder how the leaded-light windows had any glass panes left in them.

Hero! The word echoed inside Nicolo's head, mocking him, taunting him. He sank down onto a chair and thumped his fist on the desk. Sophie did not know the truth. No one did, apart from his family. The newspaper reports about the fire in his father's penthouse suite had only told half the story. They had said that the teenage Nicolo Chatsfield had saved the life of a chambermaid trapped in the fire—but he was no goddamned hero, Nicolo thought heavily. He had been a stupid, scared little boy. It had been *he* who had caused the fire. His father had managed to keep the facts from the media, but the terrible secret had hung like a weight around Nicolo's neck for all of his adult life.

For many years he had buried the truth deep inside him and enjoyed the media spotlight, playing up to his reputation as the playboy hero. His life had been one long round of parties, champagne and a constant supply of beautiful women in his bed. He had not cared about anything other than his own selfish gratification. It was as if, after the months of suffering he had endured as his burns had slowly healed, it was somehow his right to enjoy the pleasures of the flesh that had experienced agonising pain.

For how long would he have continued to live a shallow, unprincipled life? Nicolo wondered. If the chambermaid Marissa Bisek hadn't come to him eight years ago to beg him for financial help it was likely that he would still be a degenerate womaniser. The memory of the man he had been then filled him with shame. *Dio*, he had looked at the poor chambermaid, who had been horrifically scarred in the fire and yet was pathetically grateful to him for saving her, and his world had crumbled.

Faced with the evidence of his culpability, he had been forced to acknowledge he was not the hero that everyone, including Marissa, believed. The ugly scars covering his body were his punishment for his childhood crime. After meeting Marissa he had wanted to crawl away and hide beneath a stone like the worthless creature he was. But the chambermaid's lack of self-pity shamed him further. He had realised that he had a choice. He could sit around feeling sorry for himself, or he could turn his life around and do something worthwhile.

And so he had set up a charity to help other burn victims, and for the past eight years he had devoted himself to raising funds for the charity. He wasn't a hero, Nicolo thought bleakly, but he was doing his best to atone for the sins of his past.

For a moment he tried to imagine Sophie Ashdown's reaction if he told her the truth about himself. No doubt she would be disgusted. She might even rush back to London to tell her boss that Nicolo Chatsfield had no moral right to be involved in the family's hotel business.

Nicolo was impatient for Sophie to leave Chatsfield House, yet he could not bring himself to admit the truth to her. He did not want to risk seeing the same horrified expression in her eyes that he had witnessed when she had noticed the scars on his hand. He could only imagine her reaction if she ever saw the grotesque scars that covered one side of his chest. Beneath his clothes he had the body of a beast, and he was sure Beauty would recoil from him if he ever revealed his true self to her.

CHAPTER THREE

EVIDENTLY SHE HAD touched a nerve with Nicolo when she had mentioned the fire, Sophie mused. She only knew a few sketchy details about the incident that had happened almost twenty years ago. According to the newspaper report Nicolo had risked his life to save a member of the hotel staff from the blaze but he had been severely burned.

She had no idea why he had reacted so violently to her calling him a hero. He was a complicated man, she thought with a sigh.

She had not seen him since he had stormed into his study forty-five minutes ago. The trout had taken ages to bake in the old range cooker because Sophie had forgotten to change the thermostat to a higher heat setting. The delay had given her a chance to find the guest bedroom, unpack and take a quick shower, but now her stomach was protesting that it was hours since she'd eaten a couple of apples in the car on her journey to Buckinghamshire.

'You've already had your dinner,' she told Dorcha as the wolfhound nudged her with his big head. She could not resist the appeal in his liquid eyes and gave him another dog treat. 'You're gorgeous, and so friendly—not like your bad-tempered master.'

'I'm hurt by your opinion of me,' drawled a sardonic voice.

Sophie looked across the kitchen and flushed as Nicolo strolled through the door.

'I don't think you are. I don't think you give a damn about anyone's opinion of you,' she said meditatively.

He gave a careless shrug that drew her attention to his broad shoulders. She guessed from his damp hair which fell past his collar that he had showered recently. He had changed out of jeans and boots into tailored black trousers and a white shirt with long sleeves that fell low over his wrists but did not completely hide his burned hand.

The ugly scars did not lessen the impact of his smouldering sensuality. His dark, brooding looks reminded Sophie of a Byronic hero from a nineteenth century novel. No wonder Heathcliff and Mr Rochester were regarded as archetypal sex symbols, she thought as she quickly looked away from Nicolo and took a deep breath to try and steady her racing heart.

There was an air of mystery about him, and the cynical half smile on his lips both repelled and attracted her. His arrogant, devil-may-care attitude threw out a challenge to women to try and tame him, but Sophie had a feeling that no woman ever would.

She busied herself with taking the trout from the oven and draining the potatoes over the sink. 'I didn't know if you usually eat in the kitchen or the dining room, and you weren't around to ask,' she said pointedly, 'so I decided to lay the dining table.' She picked up the plates of food. 'Can you bring the salad?'

'Are you always this bossy?' Nicolo asked drily as he followed her.

'I prefer the description "organised and efficient." It's why I'm good at my job. To be honest you could do with a bit more efficiency around here,' Sophie told him. 'The house is a mess inside, and outside it's even worse. You can't expect one cleaning lady to manage a house this size. Why don't you employ more staff to take care of Chatsfield? I'm sure you can afford to. Christos said—' She broke off when Nicolo frowned darkly.

He sat down opposite her at the dining table and leaned back in his chair, studying her from beneath heavy eyelids. 'Christos said what?'

'That you have made a fortune on the stock market. Obviously I can't tell you how to spend your money...'

'But I sense you are going to tell me anyway.'

She flushed at his sarcastic tone. 'It seems a shame to let this grand old house fall to ruin. You grew up at Chatsfield, didn't you? Surely you have happy memories of living here?'

'A few, but I also have some not so happy memories.'

Sophie looked surprised. 'I would have thought that living in a great big house with your brothers and sisters, and having the huge Chatsfield estate to play in and explore, must have been wonderful—running wild in the countryside, having picnics and coming home to your parents at the end of the day.'

'It's a nice fantasy,' Nicolo said drily, 'but my childhood wasn't as idyllic as you seem to think. My parents weren't around that much. My father was away in London running the Chatsfield Hotel business and my mother was—' he hesitated '—unwell a lot of the time.'

He guessed depression was a form of illness. When he had been a young boy he had not understood the reason for his mother's frequent crying bouts, or why she locked herself in her room and refused to see any of her children.

Memories resurfaced of him standing outside her bedroom, begging to be allowed in.

'I want to see you, Mamma. I want to hug you, and then you will stop crying.'

'Go away, Nicolo. Leave me alone.'

His mother's rejection had hurt. He had thought perhaps he had done something wrong that had made her not love him anymore. Nicolo recalled how he had spent hours sitting on the floor outside his mother's bedroom, because he had wanted to be near her.

'So who took care of all the children in place of your parents?' Sophie's voice pulled Nicolo back to the present.

'We had nannies. But none of them stayed for very long because our bad behaviour made them leave,' he admitted wryly.

The baked trout was delicious, and for a few minutes Sophie concentrated on eating, but she was curious to learn more about her reluctant host.

'What happened after you were burned in the fire?' she asked tentatively, hoping he would not react angrily to her mentioning what had obviously been a traumatic event in his life. 'Did your mother take care of you while you were recovering from your injuries?'

'She wasn't around by then.' Nicolo's jaw tightened as he relived memories that were still as raw as his burned flesh had once been. 'My mother left the family when I was twelve years old. She did not know about the fire— or if she did hear she did not care about me enough to come and visit me during the many months I spent in a specialist burns unit.'

'Oh, that's awful.' Sophie's reaction was instinctively sympathetic. She knew from Christos that Liliana Chatsfield had walked out on her husband and children and had not been seen by any of the family again. Surely if Liliana had known her son had been badly burned she would have rushed to be with him?

The circumstances were different, but she understood

what it felt like to be abandoned by a parent. True, she had remained in contact with her father after he had left. Her cancer had been in remission when James Ashdown had announced that he was leaving his wife and daughter to start a new life with his mistress. But Sophie had been devastated by her father's decision. She could imagine the sense of rejection Nicolo must have felt when he had been lying injured in hospital and had desperately needed his mother.

'You must have missed her,' she said softly, 'especially while you were in hospital.'

His expression was shuttered and Sophie had a strong sense that he disliked talking about his past.

'She couldn't have done anything to help,' he said curtly. 'I owe my recovery to the doctors and the nursing staff who looked after me. I didn't need my mother fussing around me.'

Sophie found that hard to believe. She had certainly needed her mother's support during her illness, and in a funny way her cancer had brought them closer together. While she had been growing up, her mother, Carole, had been busy with her career and Sophie had spent more time with her father. But when she had been diagnosed with cancer her mother had cut down on her work to be with Sophie while she was in hospital.

Had her father felt pushed out by the close bond that had developed between mother and daughter? Sophie wondered. Was that why he'd had an affair with another woman, which had ultimately broken up the family and broken Sophie's heart?

She pushed the thought away and focused her attention on Nicolo. He had sounded dismissive of his mother, but Sophie sensed that he was adept at hiding his emotions and, in fact, had been deeply hurt by Liliana's desertion and her failure to visit him when he had been injured.

'How did the fire at the hotel start?' she asked curiously.

'I don't know,' he growled. 'Why are you so interested? It was a long time ago. Trust me, Miss Ashdown, it is better to leave the past alone. I am growing impatient with you poking your nose into things that don't concern you.'

Oh, dear, they were back to him calling her Miss Ashdown again. Clearly the slight thaw in Nicolo's attitude towards her was over. Sophie regretted her curiosity. She had been trying to gain a better understanding of Nicolo but she'd hit a brick wall.

'I'm just wondering why you are so opposed to helping restore the Chatsfield name to what it once was,' she murmured. 'The brand used to be synonymous with elegance and good taste, but that is no longer true. Frankly, every time the Chatsfield name features in the press it is usually followed by reports of scandalous behaviour by one of your siblings.'

Ignoring Nicolo's deepening frown, Sophie continued, 'It's not surprising that your father wants to change the way the business is perceived. Gene is trying to do what is best for the Chatsfield. You might not understand the reason for some of his decisions but I truly believe he has acted the way he has because he loves his children and wants to help them. That is why he has appointed Christos as CEO. Because he thinks Christos can turn the hotel business's fortunes around. But Christos needs the support of the shareholders—which means you. Surely, out of respect for your father, you should attend the shareholders' meeting?'

'My father is to blame for many of the company's

problems,' Nicolo bit out. 'It was *his* behaviour that first tarnished the Chatsfield name, and it was because of what he did that my mother...'

'Your mother—what?' Sophie broke the tense silence that had fallen. 'And what did your father do? I don't understand.'

'You don't need to understand.' Nicolo scraped back his chair and stood up. 'None of this is any of your concern.'

'But you should be concerned,' she said intently. 'If you refuse to cooperate with Christos your father has threatened to disinherit you and withhold the allowance you receive from the Chatsfield family trust fund.'

'I don't give a damn about the bloody money.' Nicolo put his hands flat on the table in front of Sophie and leaned in close so that she was forced to meet his glittering gaze. 'Giatrakos was right about one thing. I've made a fortune on the financial markets. I don't need handouts from my father and I don't care what happens to the Chatsfield Hotel chain.'

'But you do care about your brothers and sisters, and especially Lucilla,' Sophie said intuitively. 'You say you're not interested in the Chatsfield, but Lucilla cares about it, and for her sake you should consider attending the shareholders' meeting.'

'It seems to me that the best way I can help my sister is to refuse to go along with what Christos wants. I have no problem with being a thorn in his side,' Nicolo said harshly.

He trapped Sophie's gaze and she felt swamped by the force of his powerful personality. 'You've lost the argument, Miss Ashdown, and tomorrow morning you can trot back to your boss and tell him that my answer hasn't changed. I will not be at the meeting.'

He moved abruptly away from the table and Sophie released her pent-up breath on a shaky sigh as she was freed from Nicolo's magnetic spell. She was shocked by her reaction to him. While he had been leaning across the table her eyes had zeroed in on his mouth and she had found herself fantasizing about him slanting his lips over hers. Her instincts warned her he would not be a gentle lover. There was something faintly barbaric about the stern line of his mouth and she sensed his kiss would be fiercely passionate and mercilessly demanding.

No way was she interested in Nicolo, Sophie assured herself as she watched him stride out of the room. The men she dated were liberal, open-minded and completely comfortable with equality between the sexes—definitely not the kind of men who would haul a woman over their shoulder and carry her off in the manner of a primitive heathen.

She collected up the dinner plates and carried them out to the kitchen. As she loaded the dishwasher her thoughts returned to Nicolo, and she gave a rueful sigh. She doubted he had even heard of the term *New Man*. She was annoyed by her inexplicable fascination with him. It wasn't as if she was looking for a man. She was no longer in love with Richard, but she could never forget the reason why he had ended their relationship and the hurt had not completely faded. Her inability to give Richard the family he wanted had made her feel deficient, and the sense of abandonment she had felt when he had broken off their relationship had brought back memories of how she had felt abandoned by her father.

Her attraction to Nicolo was simply sexual chemistry, Sophie reminded herself. She had no intention of giving in to the disturbing feelings he evoked in her. Dangerously sexy highwaymen were fine in historical romance novels but they had no place in real life.

Sophie did not know what had woken her. For a moment she felt disorientated. The intense darkness in her room was thick and muffling, as only the darkness of the countryside was without the gleam through the curtains of car headlamps or street lights that polluted the night sky in towns and cities. The luminous dial on her watch showed that it was 3:00 a.m. From far away she heard a low rumble of thunder. Maybe that was what had disturbed her?

She settled back down on the pillows, but now that she was awake she was conscious of strange noises in an unfamiliar house. The tick of the grandfather clock on the landing seemed overly loud, and she prayed that the scrabbling sound from the wardrobe wasn't a mouse. Her heart missed a beat as she became aware of another noise.

Someone was in her room!

She could hear heavy, panting breaths coming closer to the bed.

Tense with fear, she put out a hand and groped for the lamp on the bedside table. Her fingers came into contact with something hairy and she stifled a scream as she felt hot breath on her face.

Frantically she managed to locate the lamp switch and turned it on.

'Oh, heavens! Dorcha!' she gasped when she saw the dog. Relief flooded through her as the huge hound nuzzled her arm. 'You terrified me. I thought…'

She had thought all sorts of stupid things. Only children were worried about ghosts and things that went bump in the night, Sophie acknowledged ruefully. 'Go back to your basket,' she instructed the wolfhound. 'I'm going to try and get to sleep.'

But as she reached to turn off the lamp she heard loud shouts, followed by a dreadful groaning that chilled her blood.

It sounded as though someone, or *something*, was in terrible pain. The groaning came again and Sophie knew she had not imagined it. Apart from Dorcha, only she and Nicolo were in the house. Silence fell, and she held her breath. But then it came again, this time a cry of such raw agony that she could not bear it. Jumping out of bed, she did not waste time pulling on her dressing gown as she hurried out of her bedroom and along the landing.

She did not know where Nicolo's room was, but the groans were coming from the far end of the corridor. Sophie hesitated outside the bedroom door as another desperate cry came from within, and it occurred to her that maybe a burglar had broken into the house and was attacking Nicolo.

Swallowing, she picked up a heavy pewter vase from the bureau and, gripping it tightly, she turned the door handle.

The moon was on this side of the house and it cast faint grey light through the chink in the curtains. Sophie could make out a shadowy figure lying on the bed, but there was no one else in the room. Nicolo gave a low cry that sounded as though it had been torn from his soul. What hellish place was his mind trapped in? she wondered as she stepped farther into the room.

'Nicolo…' she said softly.

'Get out!' He shouted harshly. 'For God's sake, *go!*'

'All right, I'm going. I'm sorry.' Sophie shot out of the door, hot-faced with embarrassment. Clearly she had been wrong and he hadn't been asleep and dreaming. Heaven knew why he had been making those blood-curdling groans, but she wasn't going to go back in and ask him.

She scuttled back along the landing, but his shouts followed her.

'Get out! If we don't get out, we'll die.'

Nicolo *was* asleep, and having a nightmare, Sophie realised. She was reluctant to return to his room but his harrowing cries made her turn back.

This time she entered his room and walked across to the bed. As she drew closer she saw that he was lying on his back, one arm thrown across his face. In the moon shadow she could make out his long dark hair on the pillow.

'Nicolo, wake up.'

He groaned again.

Desperate to rouse him, Sophie touched his shoulder. 'Nicolo...'

She let out a startled cry when he suddenly gripped her wrist and gave a forceful tug. Caught off balance, she fell on top of him.

'What's going on?'

'*Nicolo*—it's me, Sophie.'

'Sophie?' His deep voice was slurred.

'Sophie Ashdown—remember me? You've been dreaming....'

There was silence for a few moments. 'I grew out of wet dreams a long time ago,' he drawled finally. 'This is no dream. You feel very real to me, Sophie.'

To Sophie's shock he tightened his hold on her wrist and moved his other hand to the small of her back, pressing her down so that she was acutely conscious of his muscular body beneath her. Only the sheet and her nightdress separated them. Sophie could feel the hard sinews of his thighs. She caught her breath as she felt something else hard jab into her stomach. Nicolo was no longer caught up in a nightmare; he was awake, alert—and aroused.

She hurriedly reminded herself that it was a common phenomenon for males to wake up with an erection and it did not mean that Nicolo was responding to her in a sexual way. The same could not be said for her body, however.

'For goodness' sake, let me up,' she said sharply, frantically trying to ignore the throb of desire that centred between her legs. To Sophie's horror she felt a tingling sensation in her nipples and prayed that Nicolo could not feel their betraying hard points through the sheet.

The pale gleam from the moon highlighted the hard angles of his face and the cynical curve of his mouth. Trapped against him, Sophie breathed in the spicy tang of his aftershave. It was a bold, intensely masculine fragrance that evoked an ache of longing in the pit of her stomach. Nicolo was the sexiest man she had ever met and she was shocked by her reaction to his potent masculinity. 'You *were* having a nightmare,' she insisted. 'I was trying to wake you. What other possible reason would I have for coming to your room in the middle of the night?'

She flung out a hand and by lucky chance found the switch on the bedside lamp. Nicolo blinked in the sudden brightness and his brows lifted in surprise when he saw the pewter vase in her other hand.

'Were you were planning to do some flower arranging, or knock me out with that thing?'

Sophie flushed, wondering how she had forgotten she was holding the vase. 'I thought you were being attacked by a burglar,' she muttered.

'And you came to defend me? I'm touched.'

The mockery in his voice was the last straw. Using all her strength, she jerked out of his grasp and slid off him.

Nicolo sat up, and the sheet slipped down his body. His sardonic smile faded when he heard her swiftly indrawn breath, and following her gaze he glanced down at his chest covered in mottled red scars that ran from his hip up to his neck.

His eyes narrowed as he saw Sophie recoil from him. 'I apologise if my appearance revolts you,' he said harshly. 'Perhaps you'll think twice in future about stealing into a stranger's bedroom without invitation.'

She swallowed, desperately trying to disguise her shocked reaction to the sight of the terrible scarring that covered the left side of his torso and the whole of his arm.

'I didn't steal in here. I heard you shout out in your sleep and was concerned and came to wake you.'

He gave a grim laugh. 'And you discovered a monster. I hope the sight of my ugliness doesn't give *you* nightmares.'

'You're not a monster,' Sophie said shakily. 'I'm not revolted by your scars. But I hadn't realised the extent of your injuries. You must have been in agony in the aftermath of the fire.'

Nicolo instinctively rejected the sympathy he could see in her hazel eyes. He despised pity. In the almost two decades since he had been burned, countless women had seen him naked. He had grown used to witnessing the horror in their eyes when they saw his scars and he told himself he did not give a damn that Sophie looked sickened by the sight of his damaged body.

'I don't want your concern,' he growled. 'I suggest you get out of my room before the sight of you in your very fetching night attire makes me forget that I'm a gentleman.'

His mocking taunt reminded Sophie that she was only wearing a peach satin nightdress. Her nightwear was not especially revealing, but the gleam in Nicolo's eyes made her feel as if she'd shimmied into his room wearing nipple tassels and a thong! Flushing, she crossed her arms defensively over her breasts.

'If you were a gentleman you wouldn't have thrown me out of the house like a bag of rubbish,' she said tightly. She marched over to the door, but the memory of his desperate groans during his nightmare made her hesitate. 'Do you need anything to help you sleep?'

His low, sexy laugh sent a frisson of awareness through Sophie. 'What did you have in mind, Miss Ashdown?'

'A mallet,' she said through gritted teeth, and stalked out of the room before she gave in to temptation and hit him over the head with the pewter vase.

After Sophie had gone Nicolo switched off the bedside lamp and stared into the darkness, trying to clear his mind of the remnants of his dream. His nightmares were not so frequent now, unlike the months and years following the fire when he had suffered almost nightly flashbacks.

Sophie had been right to guess that his injuries had been agonising. It was impossible to explain the intense pain of third-degree burns that turned flesh into raw, weeping wounds, or the gut-wrenching agony of surgical dressings being changed. He had been in hospital for months and had undergone several skin grafts. Even after he had been allowed home he'd had to wear compression bandages and take high doses of antibiotics to prevent his burns becoming infected, as had happened to his friend Michael.

Nicolo closed his eyes and pictured the smiling face of the young man who had been a fellow patient at the specialist burns unit. Michael Morris had been amazingly cheerful, despite having suffered burns to eighty per cent of his body. He had been Nicolo's inspiration. But Michael had developed an infection and septicaemia and his sudden, shocking death had plunged the thirteen-year-old Nicolo into the depths of despair. He had cried like a baby when one of the nurses had told him that Michael had died.

Muttering a curse, Nicolo sat up, switched the lamp back on and picked up a book from the bedside table. Goddamn Sophie Ashdown, he thought grimly. Her arrival had unsettled him and her curiosity about the fire had opened a door in his mind that he usually kept bolted shut.

At least she had not been wearing the Chatsfield signature scent tonight. While he had still been half-asleep and disorientated he had pulled her down onto the bed and inhaled a fresh, citrus fragrance on her skin. Now the scent of her perfume lingered in his bedroom, a reminder of her enticingly curvaceous body that had not been adequately concealed by her nightgown. He imagined sliding his hands over the slip of peach silk and exploring her tantalising contours that promised to be even more sensual if she were naked.

Frowning grimly at the direction his thoughts were taking, Nicolo opened the book and forced himself to concentrate on the tale of political intrigue.

CHAPTER FOUR

Sophie leaned back in the chair and massaged her stiff neck. She had spent the morning in Gene Chatsfield's office in the west wing of the house, sorting through piles of paperwork and old files and searching for the documents Christos had asked her to find. But after three hours of solid work, she had not found anything relating to a property in Italy. Gene had not been the tidiest or most organised of men and his filing system had been chaotic, she thought ruefully.

The glorious sunshine outside the window was a temptation she could no longer ignore. It wouldn't hurt to take a break. She decided to make a sandwich and eat it while she explored the grounds. Christos had mentioned there was a swimming pool and she was keen to find it.

As she crossed the hall she heard Nicolo's voice from behind the door of his study and guessed he was speaking on the phone. He hadn't appeared at breakfast and she wondered if he would tear himself away from his computer at any point during the day. He seemed to be obsessed with making money but less interested in spending it, at least on maintaining Chatsfield House.

Twenty minutes later, when Sophie found the swimming pool, she told herself she should not be disappointed that it was unusable. The secluded area of the garden where the pool was situated looked like a wilderness and the pool was full of stagnant brown water and covered by a thick layer of green weed and algae. Weeds were growing between the tiles on the terrace that surrounded the pool and, like the house, there was an air of abandonment about the place.

What a pity Nicolo did not look after his family's home, Sophie thought. She knelt down by the edge of the pool and peered into the murky depths. It was possible that pond creatures had taken up residence beneath the dead leaves floating on the surface. Just as the thought came into her head something jumped out of the water and she gave a startled scream when a frog landed in her lap. Having lived in a town all her life, Sophie preferred to admire nature's wildlife from a distance. Gingerly she tried to flip the frog off her leg but it jumped and she gave another scream, terrified that it had become tangled in her hair.

The sound of laughter made her spin round to see Nicolo surveying the scene with amused eyes.

'Stop flapping your arms,' he drawled as he came closer. 'The poor frog is more scared of you than you are of it.'

'I wouldn't count on it,' Sophie muttered. 'Stop laughing, damn you.'

Infuriated that he clearly found the situation funny, she pushed him. He gave a grunt of surprise as he was caught off balance. His feet slid on the slippery, algae-covered tiles and he plunged into the water.

Sophie stared in shock as ripples spread across the pool. She'd hardly touched him and hadn't expected him to actually fall in. Feeling guilty, she waited by the edge of the pool for him to reappear, but as seconds ticked past and his head did not emerge through the layer of green scum she grew anxious and knelt down to try and spot him.

'That's just brilliant, Sophie,' she muttered to herself. 'You've killed him.'

She leaned forward, frantically scanning the pool for a sign of him. A hand suddenly shot through the surface and caught hold of her arm. She had no time to do more than let out a startled squeak as she was dragged down into the stagnant water.

'Oh, God, that tastes foul!' Sophie resurfaced, coughing and spluttering. Disturbing the water had produced a stench like rotten eggs and she gagged as she swam to the edge of the pool. Nicolo had already climbed out and was standing on the pool side. Leaning down, he extended a hand and pulled her up beside him.

'I've got weed in my hair—' she shuddered '—and maybe tadpoles. *Ooh*, that water is disgusting. My clothes are ruined.' Her pale blue silk shirt-dress and her beloved nude suede kitten heels would never recover, she thought regretfully.

She gave Nicolo a rueful look and silently acknowledged that, dripping wet, he looked unbelievably sexy. His sodden shirt moulded his torso so that she could clearly see the outline of his abdominal muscles, and his wet trousers clung to his powerful thighs and left little to her imagination.

She sighed. 'I guess I deserved that.'

Nicolo surveyed her through narrowed eyes. He regretted losing his temper and pulling her into the pool. But as he had helped her climb back out it had occurred to him that a dunking in the disgusting water might persuade her to give up her quest and go home. To his astonishment she did not seem about to leave Chatsfield

House in high dudgeon. Nicolo was beginning to realise that Sophie Ashdown was not a quitter.

'Please accept my apology for pulling you in,' he said gruffly. A wry smile curved his lips. 'I'm surprised you haven't tried out some tae kwon do moves on me.'

'I'd probably injure you, and dent your ego,' Sophie told him coolly.

'Why, you…' He frowned, but then his lips twitched and he threw back his head and laughed, breaking the tension between them. 'You are something else, Miss Ashdown,' he murmured with a note of genuine admiration in his voice.

Sophie felt a shaft of pleasure. She had told herself she did not care that Nicolo clearly resented her presence in his home, but the fact that his granite-like features had softened and he was actually smiling at her sent a tingle right down to her toes.

Maybe the tingle had more to do with the way he was looking at her, she conceded as she glanced down and discovered that her wet clothes were clinging to her body. She flushed when she saw her nipples were clearly visible beneath her dress and seamless bra. Nicolo gave her a sardonic look when she shivered theatrically and murmured, 'I'm cold.'

'In that case you had better go back to the house and get under a hot shower,' he said drily. 'I'll reimburse you for your clothes as your unplanned swim was my fault.'

They walked across the garden in silence. Sophie was acutely aware of him and almost wished that they were still in a state of warfare, because a friendlier Nicolo was dangerous to her peace of mind. He could be charming when he chose to be, and she sensed it would be easy to be bewitched by his charisma.

They reached the kitchen door and he stood to one side

to usher her through. Sophie brushed past him in the narrow space and as her breasts grazed his chest she could not control the tremor that ran through her.

'The water in the pool was rank. You don't smell too sweet,' he drawled.

She flashed him an angry glance. 'Neither do you.'

Too late she realised he had been goading her. He trapped her gaze and her breath left her in a rush as she stared at his hard-boned features. There was something innately sensual about his chiselled cheekbones, resolute jaw and stern mouth. Her stomach dipped as he lifted his hand and brushed strands of wet hair back from her face. Time seemed to stand still and Sophie's breathing was suddenly uneven as Nicolo stared into her eyes.

Why was he allowing this annoying woman to turn his pleasant, calm existence into chaos? Nicolo asked himself. He had spent a restless night, but he knew his inability to sleep had been the result of Sophie's visit to his bedroom rather than any lingering effects from his nightmare.

This morning he had decided that she would have to leave Chatsfield House. She was a distraction and he did not want her around. But while he had been working at his computer he had caught sight of her through the study window and his concentration had been shot to pieces. As he had watched her, a light wind had tugged on her dress and moulded the silky material to her firm breasts and slender thighs. Her honey-blonde hair rippling halfway down her back had lifted in the breeze. Reluctantly Nicolo had admitted that he was intrigued by her and, cursing his own stupidity, had followed the route she had taken through the garden.

Now he could not drag his eyes from her delicate features. His gaze lingered on her soft mouth and he felt a sharp tug in his groin.

'Curious,' he murmured. 'I've never been tempted to kiss a woman covered in green slime before.'

Beneath Nicolo's teasing tone Sophie heard something that made her heart jolt. The gleam in his eyes was blatantly sexual.

She swallowed. 'Are you suggesting that you're tempted to kiss me?'

'Do you want me to?'

Nicolo's voice was as rich and deep as crushed velvet. Sophie had never felt so intensely aware of a man, or of her own sensuality. Her mouth felt dry and she could not formulate a reply. She could hear her blood thundering in her ears, echoing the painful thud of her heart. Her brain told her she would be mad to say yes to the question, but her body was sending out a different message.

He moved his hand away from her face and Sophie's eyes were drawn to his mottled and scarred skin. She sensed he would always be haunted by the memories of that fateful night. He had been barely more than a boy at the time, a boy who had been in desperate need of his mother's love and care. It was little wonder that as an adult he was so self-contained, she thought, feeling a flare of compassion for him.

Nicolo's eyes narrowed as he watched Sophie's expressive face. He was sure he saw revulsion in her eyes when she looked at his scarred flesh.

He dropped his hand to his side and gave a grim laugh. 'Of course you don't. Why would Beauty want to kiss the Beast?' Abruptly he walked past her and strode across the kitchen to the door leading to the hall.

'I don't think of you as a beast....' Her shaky voice made Nicolo pause and swing round to face her.

'I wouldn't blame you for doing so. For a long time I could not bear to look at my reflection in a mirror and when I did finally look I was appalled by my appearance. Don't worry about it, Sophie,' he said, his tone softening when he saw her stricken expression. 'I've come to terms with my injuries, and I'm comfortable in my own skin.' He glanced down at his wet clothes. 'I'm going to take a shower and I suggest you do the same.'

Sophie had to scrub her hair to get rid of the smell of the stagnant pool water. Although she left her suede shoes to soak she did not hold out much hope that she would be able to wear them again. But her sense of fairness reminded her that she only had herself to blame. Nicolo had not invited her to Chatsfield House and since she'd arrived she had done nothing but annoy him. If she was to stand any chance of persuading him to attend the shareholders' meeting she would have to change her strategy.

These thoughts were running through her mind when she returned to the kitchen and took the bread dough she had made earlier from the bottom shelf of the range where she had left it to prove. Knocking the air back out of the dough was therapeutic. As she placed the loaf in the oven to cook, an elderly woman entered the kitchen through the back door.

'Mary at the village store said that Mr Nicolo had taken on a new cook,' the woman said to Sophie. 'I'm Betty. I dust and hoover the downstairs rooms. I can't manage more than that with my bad knees.'

'I'm sure you do a wonderful job,' Sophie assured the cleaner. Deciding not to give a complicated explanation of the reason she was at Chatsfield House, she smiled at Betty. 'When did Mr Nicolo's previous cook leave?'

'The Pearsons retired six months ago. Elsie was the

cook, and Stan was the gardener.' Betty shook her head. 'The lawn was Stan's pride and joy. He'd be horrified if he saw the mess the place is in now. The Pearsons worked at Chatsfield for years, ever since the family moved here. I've been here almost as long. Mrs Chatsfield took me on when Mr Nicolo was a baby. Mind you, there were a lot more staff then. The house and grounds were beautifully kept.'

'So you watched the Chatsfield children grow up?'

Betty nodded. 'They were a happy family at first, but things changed after Mrs Chatsfield miscarried when Mr Nicolo and Mr Franco were very young. She was devastated and was soon expecting again—too soon if you ask me! That's when she had the twins, but she suffered what used to be called the baby blues. I believe postnatal depression is the proper name for it. She used to spend hours in her room, crying, and the older children had to take care of the younger ones.'.

'I suppose their father was away working in London,' Sophie mused.

Betty gave a snort. 'Maybe he was busy running his hotels, but there was talk that he had affairs with other women. Oh, he was careful. The newspapers never got wind of what he was up to, but we heard the rumours and Mrs Chatsfield must have known about them. She persuaded Mr Chatsfield to come back to live at the house. Then Miss Cara was born. After that Mrs Chatsfield just didn't seem able to cope any more. Mr Chatsfield had gone back to London and then one day Mrs Chatsfield drove away from the house and no one ever saw her again.'

Sophie was fascinated by Betty's memories of the Chatsfield family. 'It must have been a terrible shock for the children to be abandoned by their mother.'

'It was a tragedy. The older ones had to more or less become parents to their younger brothers and sister. All the children suffered, but I think Mr Nicolo was especially close to his mother and he was badly affected by her leaving. I used to hear him crying in his room sometimes. Poor boy, he was burned to a frazzle in that fire and left with horrible scars. It was such a shame when he used to be so handsome. But he only had himself to blame.'

'What do you mean?' Sophie frowned. 'Nicolo saved someone from the flames. He was a hero—wasn't he?'

Betty pursed her lips. 'I'm not saying he wasn't brave. But Mr Nicolo had a wild streak when he was younger and there's more to the story of the fire than the newspapers ever knew. Heavens!' She broke off suddenly. 'Look at the time! I mustn't stand here chatting all day.' The cleaner made a show of glancing at the clock. She had clearly decided that she had said too much and hurried out of the kitchen clutching a duster and a tin of furniture polish.

Sophie gave a frustrated sigh as she pummelled a second batch of bread dough. She was tempted to go after Betty and demand an explanation, but of course she couldn't. The cleaning lady's words kept running through her mind. She had seemed to suggest that Nicolo was in some way to blame for the fire at the Chatsfield Hotel. It was a puzzling mystery and Sophie's curiosity longed for answers but she did not dare ask Nicolo.

He strolled into the kitchen at that moment and her thoughts were distracted by his powerful masculinity. He was wearing a pair of his customary black trousers and a loose-fitting fine silk shirt with wide sleeves that partially hid his scarred hand. Her eyes flew to his lean face and awareness uncoiled in the pit of her stomach. Betty had described Nicolo as having been handsome before he had been injured in the fire, but in Sophie's opinion he was the sexiest man she had ever laid eyes on. His face had not been burned, and apart from his hand, his clothed body bore no signs of his injuries.

Beneath his clothes it was a different matter. She *had* been shocked by his scars when she had seen his naked chest last night, Sophie acknowledged. But Nicolo's description of himself as a beast was surprising. Before he had dropped out of the media spotlight he had been a notorious playboy and he must have been aware that women found him attractive.

'I thought I could smell homemade bread. Is there no end to your talents, Sophie?' he drawled.

She shrugged. 'I enjoy cooking. I find it a relaxing pastime, especially now that I work for Christos. The man is practically a workaholic,' she said with a sigh.

'When did you start working for Giatrakos?'

'A few months ago. Before that I was PA to the director of an international car manufacturing company that has a factory in Japan. I frequently used to visit the Far East with my then-boss.'

'Japan is a fascinating country, isn't it? Did any of your trips coincide with the cherry blossom season?'

'Unfortunately not, but I've heard that the cherry trees in bloom are a spectacular sight.' Sophie looked at him curiously. 'Have you been to Japan?'

'Many times for business. Much of my financial trading is with the Asian markets and I visit Japan and Hong Kong regularly. I usually manage to fit in some sightseeing during my trips.'

'But Christos told me you rarely leave Chatsfield House.'

The moment she had spoken, Sophie wished she had

kept quiet. Her worry that she had alienated Nicolo was confirmed when he frowned.

'Giatrakos knows nothing about me. I'm not likely to confide in the enemy,' he said drily.

Heeding the warning glint in Nicolo's eyes, she dropped the thorny subject of the new CEO of the Chatsfield and turned her attention to fitting the dough into a tin.

'So who taught you to cook?' Nicolo said after a few minutes. 'Your mother?'

'Goodness, no.' She laughed. 'My mother can't boil an egg. When I was growing up she was a top lawyer and far more interested in her career than anything as domesticated as cooking. Luckily for her she married a chef.'

'So your interest in cooking comes from your father?'

'Oh—no, my father is an architect.' Sophie felt a familiar pang as she thought of her father. 'My parents are divorced,' she explained. 'Mum married Giraud four years ago, and to everyone's surprise she gave up her career and moved to Paris to help him run his restaurant.'

Nicolo glanced at her, wondering why her voice had sounded flat when she had mentioned her father. Maybe there were issues to do with her parents' divorce. He reminded himself that he wasn't interested in Sophie's personal life.

'You asked who taught me to cook?' she said after a moment. 'I learned a lot from a wonderful Italian au pair who stayed with us for a couple of years. Donatella trained to become a professional chef and she now teaches at a cookery school in Tuscany.'

She glanced at Nicolo. 'Italy is a beautiful country. Did you spend much time in your mother's homeland when you were a child?'

'We visited a few times, but my mother made England

her home with my father.' His voice roughened. 'I expect Christos told you that my mother left the family many years ago. Her whereabouts are unknown, but when I was a child she often spoke about Italy, and it is possible that she returned to her birth country.

'Italy is certainly very beautiful,' he continued. 'My villa on the shores of Lake Como has spectacular views.'

'I didn't know you have a house in Italy.' Sophie could not hide her surprise.

'Why should you? Giatrakos knows nothing about my private life,' Nicolo said drily.

From what Christos had told her, Sophie had assumed that Nicolo lived a reclusive life, but in fact he travelled regularly. She was curious about his personal life. Did he have a mistress? Perhaps he had several. He might have disappeared off the radar of the British press, but he was a virile man in the prime of his life and it was unlikely that he lived like a monk. Inexplicably, Sophie disliked the idea that he might still have numerous affairs.

She focused on what he had revealed about himself, and also the things he *hadn't* said, like how he had felt when his mother had abandoned her children. Sophie had heard a note of raw emotion in his voice, and she recalled how the cleaning lady, Betty, had said she had often heard the teenage Nicolo crying after his mother had left.

'Do you keep a house by Lake Como in case your mother *is* in Italy and you hope that perhaps one day she will look for you?' she asked softly.

Sophie's startling insight was too close to the truth for Nicolo's comfort. He had never acknowledged even to himself that he clung to the hope he would see his mother again, or that he had bought the villa on the shores of Lake Como because he felt a link to her when he stayed there.

'Don't be absurd,' he snapped. 'I bought the villa because it was a good financial investment, and also because the secluded location ensures my privacy from the paparazzi.'

Did he want privacy so that he could invite women to his house in Italy without the press finding out? It was none of her business, Sophie reminded herself. She did not care if he had half a dozen mistresses.

'I need to go and do some work,' he said curtly.

His mood swings were as mercurial as the weather, she thought, glancing out of the window to see that the sun had disappeared behind thick clouds.

'Take a slice of bread with you. It's delicious when it's still warm from the oven.' She cut two thick slices from the freshly baked loaf and spread both liberally with butter before handing him one piece.

'Mmm, heavenly,' she murmured as she took a bite of her slice of bread.

Nicolo watched her with amused eyes. 'It's refreshing to meet a woman who enjoys food. Most women seem to survive on lettuce leaves, and still worry about putting on weight. Not that you need to be concerned about that,' he added, eyeing Sophie's slender figure. 'You're perfectly proportioned.'

He visualised her when he had pulled her out of the pool. Her sodden silk dress had clung to her body, moulding the firm mounds of her breasts and her pebble-hard nipples. The jeans and T-shirt she was wearing now were not as revealing, but Nicolo felt a slow burn of desire in his gut.

'I love good food,' Sophie admitted. 'I guess I appreciate it more because for a long time I couldn't eat properly—' She broke off abruptly when she noticed the curious look Nicolo gave her and silently cursed her runaway tongue.

'Why couldn't you eat?'

'Oh…I just had a few health problems when I was a teenager,' she said dismissively. She did not want to mention her battle with cancer to a virtual stranger.

The timing of when to explain to a new acquaintance that she had once developed a life-threatening illness which had had life-changing consequences was a perennial problem, Sophie thought ruefully. Richard had accused her of deliberately withholding the fact that cancer had left her infertile. He'd said that if she had told him soon after they had met, he would not have allowed their relationship to develop, because he wanted children in the future.

It was three years since she and Richard had broken up, and the last Sophie had heard was that he had married someone else and he and his wife were expecting their first child. Since then she had dated other men occasionally, but nothing serious. She had accepted that she would probably never have her own family. Cancer, or more specifically chemotherapy, had destroyed her chance of having children. But her illness had made Sophie a realist. Life didn't come with guarantees. Rather than grieve for what she didn't have, she was grateful to be alive and determined to live her life to the fullest.

She realised that Nicolo was waiting for her to finish what she had been saying. There was no likelihood of her ever having a relationship with him—she smiled wryly at such a crazy thought—and therefore no reason to tell him about her past. 'My health is absolutely fine now,' she said cheerfully. 'What do you think of my bread?'

'It's very good.' Nicolo took a bite of warm wholemeal bread and was reminded of a field of wheat rippling in the breeze on a hot summer's day.

He sensed that Sophie had not told him the complete

story about her health problems when she had been younger. He wondered if she had suffered from an eating disorder as a teenager. She had mentioned that her parents were divorced. Perhaps the breakup had been another pressure she'd had to cope with at a vulnerable age. He remembered how angry and confused he had felt as a teenager when his parents' marriage had fallen apart.

It had been his father's fault, Nicolo thought bitterly. His father had betrayed his mother and that was why she had left. Now Gene had betrayed his children by putting an outsider in place as CEO of the Chatsfield. But if his father and the Greek usurper Giatrakos expected him to cooperate they were going to be disappointed, just as Sophie was going to be when she failed to persuade him to attend the shareholders' meeting.

CHAPTER FIVE

Sophie gave the casserole a final stir and checked that the roast potatoes were crisping up nicely on the top shelf of the oven. If the meal she had spent all afternoon preparing did not put Nicolo in a more receptive frame of mind she did not know what would. She had decided to appeal to his conscience and try and convince him that it would be in everyone's best interest, especially his sister Lucilla's, if he agreed to be present at the shareholders' meeting. She was through with prevaricating, Sophie thought firmly. She needed to use all her persuasive powers, and the dinner was part of her strategy.

The dining table looked lovely covered in a white damask cloth with a vase of roses she had picked from the garden as a centrepiece. She had even unearthed some candles from one of the kitchen cupboards and placed them in the silver candelabra that she had found.

Before serving dinner she walked into the hall to check her appearance in the mirror. Her black silk-jersey dress was elegant and businesslike and she felt confident that she deserved Christos's faith in her. Hopefully she would be able to return to London tomorrow with the news that Nicolo had agreed to play ball.

He walked out of his study, and Sophie's heart did an annoying little skitter as her eyes drank in his appearance—

black tailored trousers that hugged his hips, and a white silk collarless shirt with long sleeves. Despite his formal clothes he still reminded her of a highwayman with his dark hair falling to his shoulders and the shadow of black stubble on his jaw. It was such a resolute jaw, and Sophie suddenly felt less confident of her persuasive abilities.

She hid her reservations behind a bright smile. 'I'm just about to serve dinner. Is chicken-and-white-wine casserole okay?'

'It certainly smells good, but to be honest, anything will make a welcome change from steak.'

'Is steak really all you ever cook for yourself?'

'It's the only thing I know *how* to cook. Anyway, having the same thing for dinner every day is easier than wasting time trying to decide what to eat when I could be working.'

Sophie shook her head. 'Is making money so important to you that you don't ever take time to…I don't know—' she shrugged '—smell the roses, watch the sunset, listen to a blackbird's song? Surely life is to be enjoyed? That's especially true for people like us.'

Nicolo stared at her. 'What do you mean—people like us?'

She almost said, *People like us who have been given a second chance at life.* They had both looked death in the face and survived. But she did not want to think of the darkest days of her illness. She had felt so scared and alone when she had been in hospital for months, but she had learned to put on a brave front so that she did not upset her mother. Hiding her true feelings behind a veneer of cheerfulness had become part of her nature and she rarely shared her emotions even with her closest friends.

'What I mean is that we're lucky we don't live in a

war zone or have to cope with terrible hardship. We are healthy, and able to live our lives however we choose.'

Sophie's brand of relentless optimism was beginning to grate on Nicolo's nerves. 'Do you think I was lucky to have been severely burned in a fire?'

'No, but I think you are lucky to have recovered from your injuries and can lead a normal life. Don't you agree?'

He felt a stab of guilt as he remembered Michael, who hadn't recovered from terrible burns. Through his charity that supported burns victims Nicolo had met many people whose lives had been changed for ever by their injuries. Compared to them, of course he was lucky, he acknowledged. But he did not need a young woman who would no doubt consider breaking one of her perfectly manicured fingernails a major trauma to tell him how he should feel.

Sophie walked into the dining room. Nicolo glanced through the doorway and tensed when he noticed the candelabra standing in the centre of the table. A box of matches was on the table and as Sophie struck a match and lit a candle Nicolo jerked forward and pinched out the flame with his fingers.

'What the hell are you doing?' he growled, snatching the box of matches out of her hand. 'Where did you find the candles? I don't allow them in the house.'

Sophie stared at him in surprise, her anger at his overbearing behaviour changing to confusion when she saw his clenched jaw. She was sure she had glimpsed fear in his eyes for a few seconds.

'Th-they were at the back of one of the kitchen cupboards,' she stammered. 'Why shouldn't I light them? What's the harm in having candles on the dining table, for heaven's sake?'

'Do you know how many house fires are caused by lit candles left unattended?' he said grimly.

'I wasn't going to leave them unattended. Well—only for a few minutes while I went to the kitchen to serve dinner...' Sophie's voice trailed away as Nicolo's eyes flashed with fury. 'Okay, I'm sorry. I didn't know you had banned candles from the house. But really, a couple of candles are hardly a major fire risk.'

'What if a lit candle had fallen out of the holder while you were out of the room and set the tablecloth alight? You have no idea how fast flames can travel and how fierce a fire can become in a short space of time.'

In his mind Nicolo was back in his father's penthouse suite at the Chatsfield London hotel, trapped on the balcony as an inferno blazed inside, cutting off his path across the room to the door. His only chance of escape was to try and climb down from the balcony, but the ground was dizzyingly far below. He had been thirteen years old, faced with burning to death or risk falling to his death. The human instinct for survival had kicked in and he had started to climb over the balcony railing when he had heard screams from inside the penthouse.

His memories of the fire were so vivid that Nicolo could remember the acrid smell of smoke as if he were back in the penthouse now. He could feel his heart pounding as he walked over to the French doors and flung them open so that he could breathe the fresh evening air. The sweet scent of the honeysuckle growing up the wall of the house was a reminder of the sweetness of life, but he would never forget the charred smell of the burning penthouse—a smell he would forever associate with pain and death.

He remembered how the flames had scorched his skin as if it had happened yesterday, the smell of his flesh burning and the petrified expression on the face of the hotel chambermaid whom he had discovered cowering in the bathroom. Sophie could not comprehend the sheer terror of being trapped in a fire, he thought darkly.

'Well, I still think you're overreacting,' she muttered.

Nicolo was infuriated by Sophie's dismissive comment. 'What if a fire had started and quickly raged out of control throughout the entire house? What if one of us had been upstairs? How do you think it feels to be trapped on the upper floor with no way out, forced to watch the flames coming nearer and feeling your skin blister from the heat?'

Sophie stared at him, too shocked by the raw emotion in his voice to speak.

'I'll tell you how I felt when I was caught in a fire,' Nicolo said harshly. 'I felt sick with a fear greater than anything I could ever have imagined. I thought I was going to die—' his voice roughened '—and for a long time afterwards, when I was in agony from my burns and repelled by the sight of my scarred body, I almost wished that I had.'

He gripped the front of his shirt and ripped it open, buttons flying into the air as he wrenched the material apart to expose the red, mottled skin that covered half of his chest. '*This* is the harm a fire can inflict,' he told Sophie. 'My scars look ugly nearly two decades after I was burned. Be thankful you did not see them when they were raw and weeping.'

Last night, when she had gone to his room to wake him from his nightmare, Sophie had seen his scars in the soft light of the bedside lamp. Now, in the bright glare of the evening sunlight gleaming through the windows, the extent of his scarring was apparent. The skin on one side of his torso was mottled and discoloured, and although dark hairs covered the rest of his chest, they did not grow on the scarred area.

Nicolo's jaw clenched as he watched various expressions cross Sophie's face, the look of horror she could not disguise. He felt ashamed of his ugliness and wounded by the disgust he was sure he could see in her eyes. What had he expected? he asked himself bitterly. Of course she was repelled by his scars. He told himself he did not care. After all, she was on the enemy's side, sent here by the Greek usurper, Christos Giatrakos. Yet inexplicably, he found himself wishing that she could see beyond his scars to the man beneath.

'*Now* do you understand the destructive force of fire, and the horrific injuries it can inflict?' he demanded.

Sophie heard pain in his voice and felt an unexpected ache in her heart for this proud man. Nicolo had told her that he had come to terms with his injuries but she sensed he was watching her closely to gauge her reaction to his scars.

She recalled the day in her hospital room ten years ago when she had stared at her bald head in the mirror and wept because she had believed she looked ugly. All her friends were starting to go on dates with boys. What boy would want to date a girl with no hair? Sophie had thought. Eventually her hair had grown back and she had been left with no visible signs of her illness. But Nicolo would bear his scars for the rest of his life. Beneath his tough exterior she wondered if he felt vulnerable about the way he looked, as she had once done.

She wanted to reassure him that he was not a monster as he had described himself, but she knew instinctively that he would despise any hint of pity. Not knowing what to say, but wanting to somehow let him know that she understood and sympathised with his internal conflict, she walked over to him, and after a moment's hesitation she lifted her hand and placed it on the scarred side of his chest.

He flinched, but she sensed it was from surprise and not because the scar tissue was painful.

'I am truly sorry that I put the candles on the table,' she said quietly. 'I should have realised that you have terrible memories of being trapped in the fire.' She moved her fingers lightly over the ridges of scar tissue. 'Your scars must remind you of that night. But you are not defined by these marks on your body.'

Nicolo stared at her intently. Sophie noticed that his unusual two-toned eyes were almost completely green tonight and his black pupils were fathomless and seemed to be able to look into her soul.

He glanced down at her hand lying on his chest. 'Aren't you repulsed?' he said gruffly.

'No, of course not.' She held his gaze, her expression open and honest.

A soft breeze blew through the French doors, carrying the scent of honeysuckle and orange blossom in from the garden. In the silence Sophie could hear the slight unevenness of her breath. Gradually she became conscious of a subtle shift in the atmosphere between her and Nicolo, and beneath her palm she felt the hard thud of his heart.

Suddenly it seemed shockingly intimate to be touching him. She knew she should lift her hand from his chest but some invisible force was preventing her. Nicolo's eyes narrowed, as if he felt the same tension that gripped Sophie's body. He placed his hand on her shoulder and wrapped a strand of her hair around his finger.

'You have beautiful hair,' he murmured.

The compliment stirred her emotions. Never had she

been more thankful that her hair had grown back after the chemotherapy. The loss of such an important part of her femininity had devastated her confidence when she had been sixteen. Ten years later she appeared self-assured but deep down she was still the girl who had been worried that she would never have a boyfriend because she was unattractive.

Nicolo brought his other hand up to her face and cupped her jaw. Slowly he lowered his head and Sophie's stomach muscles clenched as she realised he was going to kiss her. She wanted him to. She could not deny the truth to herself. She had imagined him kissing her practically from the moment she had first seen him, and now, as she felt his warm breath on her lips, her heart slammed against her ribs.

Nicolo did not know exactly when his anger with Sophie had changed to desire. Deep down, he acknowledged that he had sensed an undercurrent of sexual awareness between them when he had carried her out of the house the previous day. Since then he had done his best to ignore her, but Sophie Ashdown was not easy to ignore. It was a long time since he had felt such a fierce urgency to kiss a woman. As a tremor ran through her, Nicolo sensed she was feeling as confused as he was.

Her hair felt like silk as he threaded his fingers into the honey-gold layers. She drew a sharp breath—as if she was about to tell him to stop—but before she could speak he lowered his head and crushed her mouth beneath his, kissing her with demanding passion.

Sophie's protest died in her throat and she dissolved at the first brush of Nicolo's lips across hers. Part of her was shocked by how quickly she had capitulated, but as he deepened the kiss and slid his arms around her, pulling her hard against him, nothing seemed to matter except that he should continue his sensual assault.

She framed his face with her hands and felt the slight abrasion of his rough jaw against her palms. He roamed his lips over her cheeks, her eyelids, before returning to her mouth and kissing her with a wild hunger that she found shockingly thrilling. Like the highwayman she had imagined him to be he was bold and determined, mercilessly taking what he wanted. The hard ridge of his arousal pressing against her pelvis left her in no doubt that he wanted her.

At last he released her lips, and as she snatched a ragged breath a tiny piece of her sanity returned. She was close to being completely swept away by Nicolo's raw passion. Her blood had turned to molten liquid in her veins and she was aware of a betraying dampness between her legs. He was moving his hands restlessly over her body, shaping the contours of her hips and sliding up to cup her breasts. She felt the warmth of his palm through her dress, and when he lightly flicked his fingers over her swollen nipples she gave a choked gasp and felt as if there was an invisible cord between her breasts and the pleasure spot between her legs.

It was all happening too fast, Sophie thought as Nicolo slanted his mouth over hers once more. The feel of his tongue pushing between her lips was intensely erotic but it crossed a line that she had mentally drawn in the sand. She was not ready for this level of intimacy. After all, they were virtual strangers. Thinking of how little she really knew about Nicolo was a stark reminder of why she had come to Chatsfield House. Christos had sent her here to carry out a specific task. What had happened to her professionalism? she asked herself scathingly.

She pulled her mouth from Nicolo's, breathing hard as

she tried to regain control of herself and the situation. He seemed unaware of her sudden hesitancy and pressed his lips to the base of her throat, trailing kisses down to the valley between her breasts. Sophie caught her breath as he slipped his fingers beneath the neckline of her dress and stroked her breast through her bra. Her body was on fire and yearned for him to push his hand beneath her bra and caress her naked flesh, but her brain had finally regained control.

'We should talk,' she said huskily, turning her head to prevent him from claiming her mouth again.

Nicolo frowned as her words pushed into his brain. He was intoxicated by the fragrance of her skin and by the honeyed throb of desire coursing through his veins.

'Talk about what?' he murmured. He did not want to talk. He wanted to make love. He tried to kid himself that the reason he was so massively turned on was because he hadn't had sex for a while. He hadn't been in a relationship for well over a year. Not that his affair with an air hostess who had worked the Heathrow to Hong Kong route had been a relationship as such. Sexual frustration had to be the reason why he was shaking like a teenager on a first date as he anticipated taking Sophie to bed, Nicolo assured himself. But deep down he knew it was something more. When Sophie had touched his scars he had felt a jolt of emotion that had been an almost physical pain. He had felt cleansed somehow by the expression in her eyes. There had been neither revulsion nor pity in her unfaltering gaze, simply an acceptance of his damaged body.

There had also been desire in her hazel eyes. The realisation that she was not about to reject him because of how he looked had allowed him to lower his barriers and give in to the hunger clawing in his gut. When he had kissed her their mutual passion had been explosive, so why was she pulling back, and what did she want to talk about that was more important than assuaging the need they both felt?

Sophie pulled out of Nicolo's arms and stepped away from him, feeling marginally more in control now that she was not pressed up against his muscular, half-naked body. The two sides of his shirt hung open and she quickly dragged her eyes from the dark hairs that arrowed down over his abdomen and disappeared beneath the waistband of his trousers.

They were both in the grip of heightened emotions and in that kind of situation people often acted rashly. No doubt that was why Nicolo had kissed her—and why she had responded to him.

It was time for a reality check, Sophie decided. 'I think we should focus on the reason I came to Chatsfield House,' she told him. 'Things will only get more complicated if we get…sidetracked.'

Nicolo's eyes narrowed. His body ached with frustration and he was in no mood to play word games. 'Sidetracked from what?' he demanded.

'From the issue of the shareholders' meeting that Christos wants you to attend.'

'You want to discuss Giatrakos *now*?' His voice was deceptively soft, dangerously soft, but Sophie did not immediately recognise his anger. She was relieved that she had managed to avert a difficult situation. If Nicolo had suggested that they should have sex she would obviously have refused and it might have made things awkward between them. She ignored the little voice inside her head which whispered that she was fooling herself. If he had kissed her one more time she would have been putty in his hands and might have agreed to any sexual demand he cared to make.

'I think we can agree that we both acted out of character tonight. Christos sent me here to persuade you to go to the meeting.'

'*Dio!* Did you come on to me in the hope of getting me to agree to jump through Giatrakos's hoop?' Bitterness congealed in the pit of Nicolo's stomach. 'Was kissing me part of your persuasion tactics?'

'*No!*' Sophie was stunned by his accusation. 'And I didn't come on to you. *You* kissed *me*.'

'At your invitation,' he bit out. 'When you touched me, when you placed your hand on my bare chest…' He had thought he had seen desire in her eyes, but now he realised he had been mistaken and her expression had been pity for his disfigurement.

Sophie had certainly fooled him with her apparently eager response when he had kissed her. He had been sure the attraction was mutual. Sickened by his stupidity Nicolo swung away from her and stepped through the open French doors onto the terrace, dragging in a lungful of the sweet air as if it could sweeten his bitter mood.

Bringing up the subject of the shareholders' meeting had been a mistake, Sophie thought ruefully. But she had done so because she had felt shaken by how Nicolo had made her feel, the passion that had blazed between them. Although she and Richard had been lovers she had never felt the same fire that had heated her blood when she had been in Nicolo's arms. She had been out of her depth with Nicolo, and had sought refuge in the safety of her job, which was the one area in which she felt totally confident of her abilities.

She followed him outside to the terrace. He was standing with his back to her, but she could tell from the rigid line of his shoulders that he was furious.

'I'll go and serve dinner. The potatoes are probably burnt to cinders....' She broke off abruptly, realising that it was tactless to talk about things being burned.

'Serve dinner for yourself by all means,' he said curtly. 'But not for me. I'm not hungry.'

Sophie bit her lip. 'But you haven't eaten all day. I'm sure you'll enjoy the casserole....'

'*Dio!* Do you ever listen, woman?' Nicolo's harsh voice cut through the air like a rapier. 'Go away and leave me in peace. Even better, do us both a favour and go back to London.'

Sophie bit her lip. 'I can't. I have to stay and look for the documents in your father's office.'

'Then let's make a deal.' Nicolo strode back across the terrace and stared down at her startled face. 'Chatsfield is a big house. You keep out of my way, and I'll keep out of yours. That should ensure we'll both be happy.'

CHAPTER SIX

AT THREE O'CLOCK the following morning Sophie was unable to sleep as she thought about Nicolo's extreme reaction when she had lit the candle. Now that she'd had time to dwell on what happened afterwards she could understand why he had accused her of kissing him in an attempt to persuade him to attend the shareholders' meeting. The passion that had blazed between them had been scorching, but she had called a halt because she had been afraid of where it might lead—Nicolo's bed had seemed a likely place, she thought ruefully.

It had been crass of her to mention Christos, she now realised. But to refute Nicolo's accusation she would have had to admit that she'd responded to his kiss because she had been unable to resist him. Nicolo aroused feelings in her that she had not felt for a long time. Even now, hours later, she could taste him, and every time she closed her eyes she pictured his chiselled face and his cynical mouth curving into a faint smile as he slanted his lips over hers.

She wondered why he had kissed her. He'd had every right to be furious with her. He obviously had a phobia of fire and even the tiny flame of a candle must have triggered terrible memories for him. Perhaps kissing her had been an outlet for his heightened adrenalin? What other explanation could there be? It was unlikely he was attracted to her when he did not even seem to like her very much.

Sophie did not know why the thought made her feel like a lead weight had settled in the pit of her stomach. The next time she saw him she would apologise to him *again* for all the trouble she had caused, but she acknowledged that her chances of persuading Nicolo to attend the shareholders' meeting were currently zero.

She was woken at seven-thirty by the sound of her phone ringing. Only one person was likely to call her so early and she did her best to sound alert when she spoke to Christos.

'I'm going to be out of the office, and so all my calls will automatically divert to your cell phone. You can manage things from Chatsfield House for a few days,' he told her before he dictated several letters for her to type up and email back to him. 'I've also emailed you a report, and a list of changes I need you to make to it. Have you found the documents I asked you to search for in Gene's office?'

'Not all of them,' Sophie admitted, flexing her wrist after taking notes in shorthand at record speed. 'I'll continue looking for them today.' She hesitated. 'I'm not having much luck with Nicolo either. He's adamant he won't show up at the meeting.'

'I'm sure you'll think of some way to persuade him,' Christos replied unhelpfully. 'I'm counting on you, Sophie. One of the reasons I picked you to be my PA is because I have complete faith in your ability to solve even the most difficult problems.'

So, no pressure, she thought drily as Christos ended the call, just the possibility that her job could be on the line if she failed to get Nicolo to the all-important meeting.

There was no sign of him downstairs and she guessed

he was already working in his study, but to her surprise the study door was open, and when she looked in, Nicolo wasn't there. Another puzzle was the car parked next to hers on the driveway. It did not belong to Nicolo. Sophie knew he drove a battered-looking Jeep around the Chatsfield estate.

Back in the room that had once been Gene's office she spent the morning typing up the letters Christos had dictated before she resumed her search for the paperwork he had asked for. At lunchtime she took a break and went to the kitchen to make a sandwich. Glancing out of the window, she was startled to see Nicolo and a woman walking across the garden.

Not just a woman, but an exceptionally beautiful woman, she noted as the brunette followed Nicolo into the kitchen.

Nicolo's eyes narrowed when he saw Sophie. He turned to his female companion.

'Beth, this is Sophie Ashdown, who is staying here for a couple of days,' he drawled in a tone as dry as Death Valley.

Before he could complete the introductions the woman stepped forward and held out her hand.

'Sophie, I'm pleased to meet you. I'm Beth Doyle—an old friend of Nicolo.'

Dorcha bounded into the kitchen and ran up to Beth. 'Hello, you big softie,' she said as she rubbed his shaggy head. 'I breed Irish wolfhounds on a farm in Ireland,' she explained to Sophie. She turned to Nicolo. 'You must visit again. Bring Dorcha—I'm sure he'd like to meet up with his mother.'

'I'll try and come soon,' he murmured.

Sophie felt a strange sensation in the pit of her stomach when she saw the affectionate look that passed between

Nicolo and Beth. They were obviously *close* friends, she thought as he slipped his arm around the young woman's shoulders.

'We had better get on with some work, as my visit is only a flying one this time,' Beth murmured.

Nicolo sent a brief glance towards Sophie. 'Have you finished sorting through the paperwork in my father's office?'

It was his unsubtle way of asking if she would be leaving Chatsfield House soon, she realised. She gave him a saccharine smile.

'I'm afraid not. It looks like I'll have to stay here for *ages* yet.'

Sophie watched him escort his friend into the study and close the door firmly behind them. If they worked together, then presumably Beth was a financial genius as well as having the stunning looks of a top model, she brooded as she returned to Gene's office and the mountain of files awaiting her attention. Her eyes felt scratchy from lack of sleep and she couldn't concentrate.

Was Beth's visit to Chatsfield House simply coincidence? she wondered. Or had he invited the beautiful woman to show Sophie that kissing her had been an aberration he did not intend to repeat?

By midafternoon the bright sunshine streaming through the windows made Gene's office feel like a greenhouse, and Sophie was wilting. She decided to take her laptop into the garden to work on the report Christos had sent her. Her skirt and blouse were sticking to her as she ran up to her bedroom and changed into a pair of shorts and a bikini top that she had brought with her expecting that she would be able to use the pool. Swimming in the algae-covered water was out of the question, but on her exploration of the grounds yesterday she had discovered a secluded area of garden that looked a pleasant place to sit in.

It was a secret garden, she thought fifteen minutes later as she opened a gate in a high wall and stepped into a charming knot garden where clipped box hedges grew in an intricate design intertwined with narrow gravel pathways. At the centre of the garden was a rectangular pool with water so clear that she could see goldfish darting beneath the lily pads.

The private garden was well maintained and Sophie wondered who took care of it. As Nicolo was the only person living at Chatsfield she guessed it must be him, but why was this little garden important to him when he did not bother with the rest of the estate? It was another puzzle to add to the many other things about him that fired Sophie's curiosity.

The scent of lavender growing in terracotta pots filled the air with a heady fragrance, and the only sound was the hum of bees busily searching for nectar. Sophie sat down on a bench and lifted her face to the sun. In a minute she would open her laptop, she promised herself, but her eyelids felt heavy and it was an effort to keep them open.

Nicolo strode through the overgrown garden, wondering where Sophie had disappeared to. Her car was parked on the driveway so she must still be at Chatsfield House, even though he had made it clear that he found her continued presence annoying. *Dio*, in the past two days she had pushed him into the weed-clogged swimming pool, and worse, when she had lit a candle she had triggered his deepest fear of fire. The woman was a menace, he thought grimly. But although he hated to admit it, she was also a threat to his peace of mind.

Beth had noticed that his concentration was not as sharp as usual and had teased him that maybe he did not find Sophie as irritating as he insisted, and that in fact he was attracted to her. He had denied it, but Beth was one of his closest friends and knew him better than anyone.

They had first met many years ago when she had visited her brother, Michael, in the burns unit where Nicolo was also being treated. Beth had been twelve when her seventeen-year-old brother had been severely burned in a house fire. Michael had told Nicolo that he was thankful his sister and mother had been out when a fire had destroyed their home. It was the last conversation Nicolo had had with the young man before he had died.

Beth had been heartbroken by her brother's death but she had continued to visit Nicolo while he was in hospital. They had kept in touch, and eight years ago she had given her full support to the Michael Morris Burns Support Foundation that Nicolo set up in her brother's name.

At least something positive had come from the horror of the penthouse fire, Nicolo brooded. But he could never escape the fact that he had been to blame and that he was responsible for destroying the chambermaid Marissa Bisek's life. No amount of money he raised for the charity could atone for his actions.

There was no point in raking over old memories, he reminded himself. The past was not somewhere he wanted to visit. He always found this a difficult time, with the anniversary of the fire looming. He felt more unsettled this year than usual, and he knew why. Sophie Ashdown stirred emotions in him that he had buried deep. She had forced him to think about his family, the Chatsfield Hotel business—and his father.

For years he had blamed his father for all the things that had gone wrong in his life. But according to Sophie,

Gene loved his children and wanted to help them. Nicolo grimaced. It was certainly true that—like him—all his brothers and sisters had gone off the rails in one way or another and had issues in their lives which needed to be resolved. But appointing a stranger as CEO of the Chatsfield had only served to alienate them still further.

His thoughts were distracted as he walked past the walled garden and noticed the gate was ajar. He pushed it open and came to an abrupt halt.

Emotions linked to his past were not the only thing Sophie stirred in him, he acknowledged derisively. Desire jackknifed through him as he studied the enticing vision of a blonde Venus, wearing tiny shorts and two triangles of material stretched across her pert breasts. Her head was resting against the back of the bench she was sitting on and her eyes were closed. He wondered if she'd had as little sleep as he'd had the previous night. His common sense told him to leave without disturbing her, but his feet were already crunching softly on the gravel path.

A shadow moved in front of the sun and Sophie's eyelids fluttered open. For a few seconds she was gripped with fear as a dark figure loomed over her, but as she shrugged off sleep and recognised Nicolo's lean, handsome face she felt a sharp tug of sexual awareness in the pit of her stomach.

'You startled me.' For some reason her voice emerged as a husky whisper—like a femme fatale from an old-fashioned movie, she thought, flushing with embarrassment. She held her hands to her hot face. 'I think I've had too much sun. It's lucky you woke me.'

Nicolo gave her a sardonic look and unsettled her even more when he sat down next to her on the bench.

'I searched the whole estate for you. I thought you said

Giatrakos urgently needs you to find the documents in my father's office?'

Sophie flared at the accusation in his voice. 'I'm not playing hooky, if that's what you're suggesting. I've spent hours sorting through Gene's filing system but I came out here to do some work on my laptop. I know you want me to leave Chatsfield House.' She tried to ignore the stupid feeling of hurt that he resented her presence. 'I promise that the second you agree to attend the shareholders' meeting I'll be on my way.'

'Then it looks like we're going to be stuck with each other indefinitely, because as I have already told you, I have no desire to play my father and Giatrakos's game,' Nicolo drawled.

Strangely, he did not sound angry, and he seemed relaxed, unlike Sophie, who was even more disconcerted when he stretched his arm out along the back of the bench and idly wound a strand of her hair around his fingers. He was wearing his usual black jeans and leather boots, and the top buttons of his shirt were undone, revealing his olive-skinned throat. With his dark hair falling past his collar and the customary stubble shading his jaw he was dangerously sexy. Sophie hoped he could not tell that her heart was beating painfully fast beneath her ribs.

'You seem edgy,' he murmured.

'I'm not edgy,' she denied quickly. 'Why should I be edgy?' The spicy scent of his aftershave teased her senses. She surreptitiously tried to slide along the bench away from him but found herself wedged up against the armrest as Nicolo splayed his legs so that his muscular thigh was pressed against hers.

'This walled garden is a sun-trap,' she said desperately as she dragged her eyes from the amused glint in his. He knew exactly what effect he was having on her, damn him! 'It reminds me of a garden I visited in Tuscany.'

'This was my mother's garden. She designed it and used to call it her little slice of Italy.'

Sophie heard pain in his voice and shot him a quick look. 'Is that why you look after it—because it reminds you of your mother?'

Nicolo stiffened. Sophie was too insightful for comfort, he thought grimly. He never spoke about his mother. Like so many painful things in his past, he kept the memories buried deep inside him. Sophie was watching him with a gentle expression in her hazel eyes, and something cracked a little inside him.

'I imagine she would be very different to the person I remember,' he said heavily. 'It's nearly twenty years since I last saw her and she would be an elderly lady now. If she is still alive.'

Sophie drew a sharp breath. 'Don't you know?'

'Many attempts to discover her whereabouts were made by my father, and later by me and the other members of my family. But my mother's disappearance is a mystery I fear will never be solved.'

'That's so sad.' Sophie felt a lump in her throat. It must be awful for all the Chatsfield children not to know if their mother was alive or dead, but particularly for Nicolo, who had obviously adored Liliana and had needed her support when he had been burned. She could only guess how desperately he must have missed his mother when she had left.

It had been bad enough when her parents had split up, Sophie thought. She had been heartbroken when her father had moved away to Scotland, but at least she had been able to visit him. Nicolo must have felt completely abandoned by his mother, and perhaps that was why he seemed so cold and remote. As a teenager his trust had been shattered by someone he loved and Sophie knew how painful that felt.

Feeling an instinctive need to show him that she understood, she put her hand on his arm and gave a gentle squeeze. 'I hope you find your mother one day.' She hesitated. 'You know your father really does care about you.'

Nicolo gave a harsh laugh and pulled his arm from beneath her fingers, silently calling himself a bloody fool, because for a few moments he had actually thought the compassion in her eyes was genuine.

'Is that another tactic to persuade me to go to the shareholders' meeting? You're wasting your time trying to tug on my heartstrings, because I don't have any.'

'I wasn't…' Sophie sighed. 'Why are you so angry with your father?'

'I have my reasons,' Nicolo said curtly. He had never told anyone the discovery he had made about his father when he had been thirteen, and he was certainly not going to reveal the secret he had kept all these years to Sophie.

He glanced at his watch. 'I came to find you to tell you that Beth and I will be eating out tonight, so if you were planning to cook you'll only need to make dinner for yourself.'

'Fine.' Her voice was as curt as his. She had forgotten about Nicolo's *friend*. She wondered how long beautiful Beth was planning to stay at Chatsfield House—and where she would be sleeping. It was none of her business if Beth was Nicolo's mistress, Sophie told herself angrily.

'Beth had intended to stay here for a couple of days—' Nicolo unknowingly answered one of Sophie's questions '—but her husband phoned to say that one of the boys is ill with suspected chickenpox. She is trying to arrange to fly back to Dublin later tonight.'

'Husband?' Sophie stared at him. 'I didn't realise Beth is married.'

'She married an Irishman. Liam is busy on their farm at this time of year and he stayed in Connemara with their two sons.'

'I thought that you and she…' She spoke unthinkingly. Realising she was giving away too much she broke off, flushing hotly.

'You thought Beth and I were in a relationship?' Nicolo frowned. 'I would not have invited a lover here the day after I kissed you. What kind of man do you think I am?'

'A few years ago you had a reputation as a playboy,' Sophie reminded him. 'Just because you're no longer pictured in the newspapers with a different woman every week doesn't mean that you might not still be a womaniser. Maybe you simply take more care to avoid the paparazzi.'

Nicolo's jaw tightened. 'There are many things in my past that I am not proud of,' he said roughly. 'I've changed from the person I was then.'

Was he saying that when he had kissed her last night he had not automatically assumed it would lead to casual sex? Sophie's brow furrowed.

'Why *did* you kiss me?' she blurted out.

'Why do you think?'

The question hung between them. His voice had changed; no longer clipped and cold, but soft and deep—like the rich, warm tones of a cello, Sophie thought. The air in the walled garden was strangely still and utterly silent so that she was sure Nicolo must be able to hear the frantic thud of her heart.

She froze as he moved his hand from the back of the bench and placed it heavily on her shoulder.

'Look at me,' he murmured.

Slowly she turned her head and found him watching her from beneath heavy lids that did not wholly hide the hard glitter in his eyes. She had seen the same predatory expression in his eyes last night, just before he had kissed her. Anticipation licked through Sophie's veins like wildfire and she unknowingly knotted her fingers together in her lap as she waited for his head to descend.

'You're not naive, Sophie. You know what is happening between us,' he said softly.

Last night Nicolo had been unable to sleep while his mind had replayed the kiss he had shared with Sophie— *shared* being the crucial word. She had responded to him with a passion that could not have been faked, and he *had* seen desire in her eyes. It had not been pity, as he had later believed.

Now he was in no doubt that it was desire darkening her hazel eyes, and as he slid his hand beneath her hair and cupped her nape he felt the tremor that shook her slender frame.

'You feel the chemistry that exists between us, just as I do,' he insisted. He sensed she was going to deny it, and before she could speak he bent his head and covered her lips with his.

'Oh.' Sophie made a muffled sound as the first touch of Nicolo's mouth sent pleasure cascading through her. He had spoken of chemistry, and that was exactly what it was, she thought dazedly. The mysterious alchemy of sexual attraction was impossible to define but it burned white-hot as he kissed her with a hunger he did not try to hide.

She closed her eyes against the glare of the sun and

her senses became attuned to the feel of his lips sliding over hers, the sensual musk of male pheromones mixed with the scent of his cologne, and the ragged sound of his breathing, *hers*, as their mutual excitement heightened.

Despite the heat in the walled garden she shivered as he trailed his mouth over her throat, her shoulder, the upper slope of one breast. She was aware only of Nicolo's strong hands on her body, his lips caressing her skin. Her breath left her in a gasp as he undid the halter ties of her bikini top and peeled the stretchy material down until he had bared her breasts.

'You're so bloody beautiful,' he said harshly. The words were like the man—bold and blunt, with a raw honesty that thrilled Sophie more than any flowery compliment could have done. He cradled her breasts in his big hands, his touch surprisingly gentle. Her flesh responded eagerly, her nipples swelling to hard points, and she gave a keening cry as he lowered his head and flicked his tongue across one peak and then the other.

Dizzy with desire and trembling with need, Sophie arched her back. 'Please...' she whispered. She curled her fingers into his thick hair as he drew one nipple into his mouth and suckled her. The sensations shooting down to her pelvis were beyond anything she had experienced before. She could hear a feral panting sound and realised it was coming from her, but as Nicolo closed his mouth around her other nipple all rational thought faded from her mind and she pressed her quivering body urgently up against him.

Nicolo shifted position to try and ease the throb of his erection straining beneath his trousers. In his mind he was imagining sliding his arousal between Sophie's slim thighs and thrusting into her, giving them the release they both craved. He knew she shared his eagerness. Her response to him was unguarded and honest, like Sophie was herself, he acknowledged. There was no pretence with Sophie. He might not like some of the things she said but did not doubt that she always spoke the truth and he trusted her integrity. The realisation shook him.

He trailed his lips over her satiny skin and claimed her mouth once again. A groan escaped him when she parted her lips and kissed him with passion and an underlying tenderness that made his gut ache. One part of his brain was debating whether he could make love to her here in the walled garden. The house was far away and it would take too long to reach his bedroom. Why not pull her down onto the cool green grass and take her now, before his body exploded with frustration?

He tried to block out the voice inside him that was urging him to show restraint and control his hunger. An unwelcome memory slid into his head of how Sophie had reminded him that he had once been a womaniser. He had told her the truth when he'd said he had changed and was no longer the man he had been in his twenties. He did not have one-night stands or treat women as playthings and he was ashamed of how he had once behaved.

So why was he planning to have sex with a woman he barely knew? Nicolo tensed. In the past few years he had clawed back a little self-respect. It was a testament to Sophie's allure that he was tempted to throw away his hard-won esteem by having casual sex with her. Because what else could it be other than a few moments of meaningless carnal pleasure? he thought grimly.

He did not want an affair with her. He was too bound to his past to be able to offer her any kind of relationship. But he felt instinctively that, for Sophie, sex would never be a casual act. Right now she was caught up in the heat of passion, and Nicolo sensed that if he took things further and made love to her in the secluded garden she would be willing. But afterwards it was likely that she would feel disappointed with herself, particularly when she realised that a brief physical union was all he wanted.

He looked down at her beautiful, rose-flushed face and felt his resistance waver when he saw the invitation in her soft, hazel eyes. *Dio*, how could it be wrong when it felt so right? He had never ached to make love to any woman the way he was aching now.

He closed his eyes and another face flashed into his mind. Marissa had suffered third-degree burns to her face in the Chatsfield penthouse fire and had been left horrifically disfigured. Ashamed of the way she looked, she hid herself away and had developed the panic disorder agoraphobia, which had made her a prisoner of her own home. On the night that Marissa had visited him at Chatsfield House she had been trembling with fear, but a desperate need for his help had forced her to overcome her panic attack.

Sophie was unaware of the terrible secret he carried, the burden of guilt about Marissa that haunted him. It would not be fair to make love to Sophie without telling her the truth about himself, and then surely she would recoil from him in horror and disgust. Nicolo gave a silent groan. How could she understand his torment? He guessed from Sophie's cheerful nature that she had never experienced a traumatic event in her life. She was like a pure, golden light that had briefly lightened his darkness and he could not bear to taint her with the blackness of his soul.

He should have listened to his common sense and left her alone in the garden. Instead he had created a situation that was fast spiralling out of control. It took all his willpower to tear his mouth from Sophie's, and guilt clawed in his gut when he saw the confusion in her eyes as he dropped his arms to his sides.

'I'm sorry,' he said brusquely, stepping away from her. 'It's not you.' He stared at her stunned face for another minute and then turned abruptly and strode along the gravel path.

CHAPTER SEVEN

THE CLICK OF the garden gate closing told Sophie that Nicolo had gone. Only then did she realise that she had been holding her breath, and she released it on a shuddering half sigh, half sob. Even though she felt utterly humiliated there was a part of her that wanted to run after him and beg him to finish what he had started. Her body was screaming for sexual release and every nerve-ending felt ultrasensitive.

It's not you, he'd said. She gave a mirthless laugh. Of course it was her fault that he had stopped making love to her. Nicolo had rejected her and the only explanation Sophie could think of was that she did not turn him on. He had aroused her with his passionate kisses, but clearly she had not excited him. Rather than embarrass her, he had made the excuse that it was not her fault. But his abrupt departure from the garden made her feel a failure as a woman.

Perhaps she lacked some vital ingredient that would induce men to stay with her, she thought bitterly. Richard had broken off their relationship because of her inability to have children, but maybe her infertility had only been part of the problem.

She glanced down at her naked breasts with their reddened, swollen nipples, and a wave of shame rolled over her as she recalled her wanton response to Nicolo. With trembling fingers she dragged her bikini top into place and tied the halter strings into a tight knot. How could she have almost had sex with a man she hardly knew? she wondered, disgusted with herself. But when Nicolo had kissed her and held her so close against his chest that she had felt the powerful beat of his heart, she'd had a strange feeling that she had known him in another life and he was her destiny.

She bit her lip. Obviously he had not shared that feeling. She could not bear to face him again. She would have to return to London and tell Christos that she had failed to persuade Nicolo to attend the shareholders' meeting. It would hurt her pride, but not as much as if she had to remain at Chatsfield House for another day, another hour.

The idea of returning to the house briefly to collect her belongings made her feel sick, but to her relief she did not see Nicolo when she slipped in through the kitchen door. Only Beth was there and she smiled when she saw Sophie.

'This has turned out to be an even shorter visit than I'd planned,' she said ruefully, indicating her suitcase standing by the door. 'One of my sons has come down with chickenpox and my husband has just phoned to tell me that Connor, our eldest, has a few suspicious-looking spots.'

'I'm sorry,' Sophie said sympathetically.

Beth laughed. 'The joys of parenthood! I must go, or I'll miss my flight. If you're wondering where Nicolo is—he's taken Dorcha for a walk.' She hesitated and gave Sophie an intent look. 'Nicolo said you'll be staying at Chatsfield House for a few more days. I'm glad you're here,' Beth continued before Sophie could explain that she intended to return to London immediately. 'It's the anniversary of the fire soon. Nicolo insists he'll be fine, but I know he has terrible memories of what happened. I'm relieved that he won't be here alone.'

'I…' Sophie did not know what to say. She was under no obligation to stay at the house, she assured herself as she watched Beth get into her car. It was unlikely Nicolo would welcome her being here at what must be a very painful time for him. Her common sense told her to leave before he came back from his walk, but her heart said something else.

She remembered the haunted expression in his eyes when he had described being trapped in the fire at the hotel. Such a horrific experience would be impossible to forget, especially when the scars on his body were a constant reminder of what he had been through.

But how could she face him after he had rejected her earlier? Thinking about how she had clung to him and offered him her body made her cringe with embarrassment.

As Nicolo walked up the garden path he smelled a tantalising aroma coming from the kitchen. Roast lamb, he guessed, cooked with herbs. He frowned. Beth had been about to leave when he'd set off for a walk over an hour ago and he did not understand why she was still here. She would not get to the airport in time for her flight.

Dorcha bounded ahead, drawn by the delicious smells. The dog whined at the kitchen door, and a few moments later it was opened—by Sophie.

Nicolo struggled to hide his shock. He had assumed she would be halfway back to London by now. She was still wearing the tiny shorts that revealed her long, tanned legs but he noted that she had replaced the sexy bikini top with a T-shirt. The shirt was loose-fitting but he could tell she wasn't wearing a bra beneath it, and the memory of caressing her naked breasts sent a jolt of desire through him.

There were not many occasions when he was lost for words but he did not know what to say to her. He realised he did not want to say anything. Talking tended to complicate things. He wished fiercely that things were different, that *he* was different. He wished he could pull her into his arms and kiss her soft mouth. Then she would put her arms around his neck and he would carry her upstairs to his bedroom and make love to her until the shadows of dusk lengthened into the velvet darkness of night.

In reality, of course, he could do no such thing. But the fantasy lingered in his mind as he followed her into the kitchen.

When Sophie saw Nicolo her composure wobbled dangerously, especially when she walked back into the kitchen and turned to find him close behind her. She silently cursed her intense awareness of him but could not prevent her eyes from lifting to search his lean face. Why did the faintly cynical curve of his lips cause her stomach to swoop as if she was riding a big dipper at a funfair? she wondered wearily.

To her surprise he avoided meeting her gaze and dull colour flared on his high cheekbones. She sensed he felt as uncomfortable as she did. Too bad, she thought. She had decided to stay until after the anniversary of the fire—although she had no intention of telling him that she was concerned about him being alone with his dark memories.

'I've prepared roast lamb, new potatoes and green beans for dinner,' she said crisply, slipping into her familiar role of superefficient personal assistant to mask her agonising awareness of him. 'I thought we'd eat in the kitchen.'

As she served the food she sought for something—anything—to say to break the tense silence.

'Beth seemed nice. She said you've been friends for many years.'

Nicolo hesitated. He had a deep-rooted dislike of talking about his past but strangely he found he wanted to tell Sophie about Michael.

'We met when she used to visit her brother in the burns unit of the hospital where I was treated,' he explained gruffly. 'Michael was badly injured in a fire that started when he left a candle burning one night. Beth and her mother had been staying with a relative and returned to find their home destroyed and Michael in intensive care. He and I became friends in hospital, but tragically Michael died of his injuries.'

'How terrible,' Sophie murmured. The story explained why Nicolo had reacted so strongly when she had put candles on the dining table. She thought of Beth's bright smile that hid such a deep personal tragedy and wondered if the close bond she had sensed between Nicolo and the young woman was because they had both experienced the utter devastation a fire could cause. Nicolo's face was shuttered and she had no idea what he was thinking, but she sensed his mood was grim and wished she had not unwittingly reminded him again of the tragedy in his own past.

She sat down opposite him at the kitchen table to begin her meal. 'I've just remembered I bought a bottle of wine while I was in the village. Would you like some with your dinner?'

'I never drink alcohol.'

She looked at him in surprise. 'Not even wine? I would have thought that being half-Italian you would enjoy drinking wine. Don't you like it?'

'I used to like it too much.' Nicolo's jaw tightened as he thought of his youth, which he had mainly spent drinking himself into oblivion. No party had been complete without his presence, and beautiful women had literally queued up for him to take them to bed. He had been out of control, on a fast track to damnation, until one night he had met the hotel chambermaid whose life he had saved—and his life had come crashing down.

He blocked out the memories—something he had grown adept at doing—and looked across the table at Sophie, wondering why he was tempted to tell her the truth about his past. She would not understand why he still felt tormented so many years after the fire, he reminded himself. He bet Miss Bright-as-a-Button had never had to cope with a traumatic event in her life.

'You ask a lot of questions,' he said curtly. 'Let me ask you some questions for a change.'

She shrugged. 'What do you want to know?' She did not have any secrets. Well, apart from one, Sophie acknowledged. But her infertility was not a subject Nicolo was likely to be interested in.

He finished eating and leaned back in his chair. 'Why did you learn tae kwon do?'

'There was a martial arts club at university. Actually, my friends and I only went along because the sports coach was good-looking and we all fancied him. Richard thought I had a natural flair for tae kwon do and offered to give me private coaching sessions.'

'Did the handsome coach remain as just your martial arts instructor?'

'No,' she admitted. 'We obviously spent a lot of time together, training and going to competitions, and our relationship developed into a personal one.'

Why the hell did he feel an irrational dislike for a man

he had never met? Nicolo asked himself irritably. So what if Sophie had the hots for her sports coach? 'Are you still in a relationship with him?' he asked in an offhand tone.

'No,' she replied flatly.

Nicolo shot her a sharp glance. 'Your choice or his?'

'His, if you must know.' She scraped back her chair and collected the used plates. 'If you want dessert there's ice cream in the freezer.'

'Were you in love with Mr Tae Kwon Do Coach?'

She dumped the plates in the sink, her back ramrod-straight. 'It's none of your business.'

'Ah, so you were.' Nicolo knew he was needling her. What he did not understand was why he was so interested in her love life. 'Why did he break up with you?'

She swung round and glared at him. *'Because...'* She took a deep breath, and said in a quieter voice, 'Because we had issues that we couldn't resolve. We wanted different things, which made it impossible for us to plan a future together.'

Her mind flashed back to the night that Richard had ended their relationship. Previously he had dropped a few hints that he saw them having a future together, and Sophie had decided she must tell him that her cancer treatment had made it unlikely she would be able to have a baby.

His reaction had been devastating.

I want children. I can't contemplate a future that doesn't include having a family. I'm sorry, Sophie, but it's how I feel. I wish you had told me sooner that you can't conceive.

They hadn't even stayed to finish their meal in the restaurant, Sophie remembered. Richard had driven her straight home. She had felt too numb with shock to cry. She had believed that Richard loved her, but he hadn't loved her enough to be able to accept her for who she was. Her inability to have children was not her fault, but she had been punished for it and rejected by the man she loved. By the second man she had loved, she amended. The first had been her father.

Swallowing hard, she concentrated on rinsing the plates under the tap before stacking them in the dishwasher.

'I'll do that.' Nicolo's deep voice sounded close and she glanced up to find him standing next to her. His physical presence was overwhelming. Her fierce awareness of him made her hot and flustered, especially when he murmured, 'Dinner was superb. Your boyfriend was a fool to give you up.'

'Unfortunately my ability to cook well wasn't enough to sustain our relationship,' she said drily.

Nicolo wasn't fooled. He sensed that the ex-boyfriend had broken her heart and he felt an irrational surge of anger for the unknown Richard. He'd only known Sophie for a short while but he had been struck by her compassion and genuine kindness, and he was certain she had not deserved to be hurt.

He lifted his hand and brushed her hair back from her face. Her skin felt as soft as a peach as he rubbed his thumb along her cheekbone. She flinched and stepped away from him, and Nicolo grimaced, aware that after he had walked away from her in the walled garden he deserved her coolness.

It was torture being here with Nicolo, Sophie thought despairingly. The scene of comfortable domesticity as they cleared up after dinner was beguiling and a painful reminder that she was unlikely to share her life with anyone. It was possible that she would one day meet a man who did not want children, but she had come to terms with the likelihood that she would never marry and have a family. Most of the time it did not bother her but tonight for some reason it hurt—a lot.

'I'll leave you to finish here,' she said abruptly. 'It's late, and I'm going to bed.'

'It's eight-thirty,' Nicolo pointed out.

'I didn't sleep well last night.'

'Not surprising perhaps, after you had nearly drowned me in my swimming pool.'

Sophie flushed. 'I've told you how much I regret that.' The gentle amusement in his eyes was more unsettling than his anger had been. 'If you must know, I regret coming to Chatsfield House at all,' she said huskily. She suddenly felt drained and emotional and feared that if she did not get away from Nicolo she might do something stupid like burst into tears. She hurried over to the door.

'Sophie…' His voice was low and rough, as if her name had been torn from his throat. She desperately wanted to turn round, but for once her common sense won over her heart and she forced her feet to keep moving out of the kitchen.

She would not miss this room when she left Chatsfield House, Sophie thought as she glanced around Gene Chatsfield's office. For the past ten days she had become a virtual prisoner in the office so that she could avoid Nicolo. At least she had finally unearthed the documents relating to the property in Italy. Surprised that it wasn't for one of the hotels, but of a private property in Italy, Sophie mused that it wasn't really any of her business anyway. After tonight—the anniversary of the fire—there would be no reason for her to prolong her visit.

After what had taken place in the walled garden she had been unable to bring herself to try and persuade him to attend the shareholders' meeting. She felt as if she was living in limbo. It would be good to go back to her flat in Covent Garden and the daily routine of working for Christos. Her life would return to normal and no doubt she would quickly forget about Nicolo Chatsfield.

Who was she kidding? Sophie thought bleakly. He dominated her thoughts day and night. Fortunately he seemed keen to avoid her too, and spent hours working in his study. The only time they met was at dinner every evening. She found cooking complicated recipes was a welcome distraction from thinking about Nicolo, but as soon as he joined her in the kitchen her tension returned as she desperately tried to hide her intense awareness of him.

She sensed that he found their stilted conversations during dinner as much of an ordeal as she did. Sometimes she would glance at him and find him watching her with an expression in his eyes that she dared not define. But she was conscious of the simmering sexual chemistry between them, and immediately after dinner she left him to clear away the dishes and made an excuse to go up to her room.

This evening she would have to ignore the awkward atmosphere and remain downstairs with Nicolo, Sophie told herself. She did not expect that he would confide in her, but she was determined not to leave him alone with his memories of the horrific fire.

An hour later she put the pot of chili con carne she had made into the oven and turned the heat setting to low. Unable to face spending any more time in Gene's office, Sophie stepped outside. It was a beautiful summer's evening and the golden rays of the sun reflected on the red bricks made the house look less like a grim Victorian institution.

She was surprised when she walked through the

grounds of the estate and found that the swimming pool had been drained and cleaned and was being refilled. What a shame it would not be ready to swim in until after she had left, Sophie mused as she strolled back to the house. She wondered if Nicolo intended to use the pool. Imagining him wearing just a pair of swim shorts sent a rush of heat through her and she told herself it was lucky she *was* leaving tomorrow, before her stupid fixation with him got out of hand.

As she crossed the garden she heard music coming from one of the rooms. The French doors of the sitting room were open and someone was playing the grand piano with an expertise and depth of emotion that made Sophie catch her breath. Listening to the sweet, pure notes made the tiny hairs on the back of her neck stand on end. Chopin was her father's favourite composer and she recognised the piece as one that she had often heard James Ashdown play when she had been a child.

She crossed the terrace and peeped into the room. It could only have been Nicolo who was playing, but she still felt a jolt of shock as she watched him move his fingers across the keys. His eyes were half-closed and she sensed he was lost in the music, as if the notes flowed through his body.

Tears filled Sophie's eyes. It seemed incredible that Nicolo, who had experienced terrible pain when he had been burned, could play with such sensitivity and produce music so beautiful that it stirred her soul.

'Come in if you want to. You don't have to hide out there.'

His voice made her jump and she flushed guiltily. As she stepped through the French doors Nicolo's fingers did not falter on the keys, and he did not glance at her as he continued playing, slipping from classical pieces to modern tunes and finally Chopin's *Nocturne*.

'Does music always make you cry?' He played the last notes of the piece and looked across the room at her, his eyes intent on her face. 'Or was my playing so bad it made you weep?' he said wryly.

'Of course not. I had no idea you could play the piano so amazingly.' Sophie quickly wiped her eyes. 'Hearing you play reminded me of my father. He is a wonderful pianist. When I was a child he used to play to me when he came home from work. I used to sit next to him and listen. He tried to teach me to play, but I'm afraid I didn't inherit his talent or his patience,' she said regretfully.

'Did he teach you to play this?' Nicolo played a tune that Sophie instantly recognised as one she had played as a duet with her father. 'It's one of the first pieces my piano teacher taught me,' Nicolo said when she nodded. 'Come and play it with me.'

He made room for Sophie on the piano stool, and after a moment's hesitation she sat down next to him. 'I don't remember how to play the tune.'

'It's not difficult. You play these notes on the higher octave—' he showed her the correct notes '—and I'll play the accompanying tune on the lower octave. Ready?'

After a couple of false starts Sophie managed her part of the duet. Memories came flooding back of sitting with her father just as she now was with Nicolo. 'Dad and I used to pretend that we were playing in a famous opera house, and when we finished the piece he would take my hand and we would bow to the audience.' She flushed. 'It sounds silly, but it was such fun.'

'It's not silly. It's good that you have such great memories of your childhood. Are you close to your father?'

'I used to be once.' Sophie bit her lip. Hearing Nicolo

playing the piano so exquisitely had stirred emotions inside her that she usually kept buried.

'When I was growing up I adored my father. My mother was busy with her law career and I spent a lot of time with Dad.' She smiled. 'I remember for my ninth birthday he designed and made me a fantastic doll's house. And he taught me how to play tennis, and chess.' Her throat ached as she recalled her happy childhood. 'Everything changed when my parents divorced.'

Sophie tried to block out the memories of the day her father had walked out of the family home for the final time. She had felt an acute sense of betrayal and had longed to run after him and plead with him to stay. Weak from months of chemotherapy, she hadn't understood how he could leave at a time when she needed his love and support. She had thought that, having beaten cancer, her life would return to normal. But as she had watched her father drive away Sophie had realised that her pre-cancer, carefree life had disappeared for ever.

'I was going through a…difficult time and I was angry with Dad for moving away when I needed him. For a long time we didn't talk.' She sighed. 'He tried to phone me, but I refused to speak to him. I guess I sound like a spoilt brat, but I was so upset that he had left.'

Sophie fell silent, wondering why she had revealed so much of herself to Nicolo of all people. She was about to get up from the piano stool when he spoke.

'I think your reaction to your father leaving was understandable,' he said gently. 'You must have felt that he had abandoned you.' His voice hardened. 'Believe me, I know how that feels. I was a very angry and confused teenager after my mother left. You said your father moved away. Where does he live?'

'In Scotland, with his new wife.' Sophie hesitated.

'He has two daughters with Janice. Kirsty and Laura are only eight and four years old.' She did not admit that she found it hard to think of her father and Janice's children as her sisters. Even harder to admit to herself was the jealousy she felt that her father's little girls had taken her place in his affections. She wondered if he taught them to play the piano.

'Your father's young daughters must love having an older half-sister,' Nicolo said. 'I expect you are very important to them in the same way that Lucilla was to me and my younger brothers and sister.'

She shrugged. 'I don't see them very often. Working for Christos is pretty full-on, and I don't get the chance to go up to Edinburgh much.'

Guilt niggled at Sophie as she thought of the last time she had visited her father and his family the previous Christmas. On the surface the visit had gone smoothly; the adults had been ultra-polite and the little girls had been sweet and touchingly friendly. But Sophie's inner tension had been mirrored in Janice's taut smile. Memories of old hurts and emotional wounds had hovered in the atmosphere, and Sophie had sensed that both her father and his wife had breathed a sigh of relief, just as she had done, when Christos had phoned and asked her to return to work early.

She jerked back to the present when she realised that Nicolo was speaking.

'It was Lucilla who suggested I should learn to play the piano.'

He had pushed his shirtsleeves up his forearms before he had started to play, and now he rested his scarred hand on the keys. His mottled, red skin made a stark contrast to the smooth white keys and Sophie could not drag her eyes from his disfigured hand, imagining how painful his injuries must have been in the weeks and months after he had been burned.

'My sister did a lot of research about burn injuries and thought that playing would be good physiotherapy for my fingers.' Nicolo played a few scales, his fingers moving effortlessly across the keys. 'Immediately after the fire I had virtually no movement in my fingers. Learning to play the piano was not just good for exercising the muscles in my hand, it also gave me a purpose—' his voice deepened '—and it helped me to cope with the pain of my burns.'

Sophie's eyes flew to his face and she guessed from his ravaged expression that he was reliving the horrors of the past.

'I know tonight is the anniversary of the fire,' she said softly. He gave her a surprised look and she explained. 'Beth told me the date. She didn't want you to be on your own this evening.'

Immediately she realised she had made a mistake. Nicolo frowned darkly. 'Did Beth ask you to stay?' His eyes flashed with anger. 'Did you remain at Chatsfield House because of some misguided idea that I might need a shoulder to cry on? *Dio*.' His lip curled sardonically. 'Who do you think you are—Mother Teresa?'

He sprang up from the piano stool and said savagely, *'I don't want your goddamned pity!'*

CHAPTER EIGHT

'I DON'T PITY YOU,' Sophie insisted as she leapt to her feet. Nicolo towered over her and she tilted her head to meet his furious gaze. 'But I don't understand you. Why do you hide away here? Why have you cut yourself off from your family, and in particular your father and the business he built up?

'Being trapped in that fire must have been terrifying, and your injuries must have been agony,' she said huskily. 'But you survived. Surely you must realise better than most people how precious life is?' Having faced death herself, she appreciated every day of her second chance at life.

'You did a wonderful thing,' Sophie continued when he made no response. 'You rescued a member of the hotel staff from the fire. You were a hero and you should be proud of what you did.'

'Proud?' Nicolo gave a bitter laugh. Sophie's words mocked him. The fire had happened so many years ago but his memories would never fade. Tonight, especially, he was filled with the self-loathing that had haunted him for almost two decades.

'I've said it before, Sophie,' he said curtly. 'You ask too many questions.' He stared at her lovely face and something cracked inside him. He did not want her here. He did not want her to look at him with gentle compassion in her eyes that made his gut ache.

'Do you want to know the truth? I was no bloody hero. It was *me* who started the fire. It was my fault that the maid was trapped in the blaze and my fault that we both nearly burned to death.'

Sophie suddenly recalled a conversation she'd had with the cleaning lady, Betty.

'Mr Nicolo had a wild streak when he was younger... there's more to the story of the fire than the newspapers ever knew....'

She glanced at Nicolo and her heart turned over when she saw his tortured expression. 'I don't understand,' she said shakily. 'How could you have started the fire?'

He raked his hand through the dark hair that fell past his collar, and despite the tension, Sophie's stomach muscles tightened with fierce sexual awareness. With his chiselled features and a hard gleam in his eyes he was the dangerous highwayman of her imagination, but she had glimpsed a softer side to him, a vulnerability that made her yearn to put her arms around his waist and lay her cheek against his chest.

'I was drunk,' he said abruptly.

'*Drunk?* You were *thirteen*.'

'I'd been drinking my father's whisky.' He exhaled heavily. 'I'd let myself into his penthouse apartment with the intention of tipping his scotch down the sink. Childish, I know, but I *was* still a child. I was feeling very angry with my father about—' his mouth tightened as he recalled how a few days earlier he had discovered his father in bed with a naked woman who Nicolo had recognised as one of the hotel chambermaids '—about something he had done,' he muttered. 'I wanted to annoy him.

'Gene owned a collection of rare and expensive malt

whiskies. I drank probably half a bottle, tipped the contents of the other bottles away and then tried smoking one of his cigars.' He grimaced. 'The damn thing tasted disgusting, and I remember I threw it in the bin before I nearly threw up.

'Soon after that I must have fallen asleep due no doubt to the effects of the alcohol. When I woke up the penthouse was engulfed in flames and I couldn't get across the room to the door. That's when I realised I was trapped.'

'It must have been terrifying,' Sophie murmured.

'My only hope of escape was to climb down the drainpipe running down the outside wall of the hotel. I was six floors up, but it was worth a try.' Nicolo shook his head. 'To be honest I doubt I would have made it, but as I was climbing over the balcony rail I heard someone screaming from inside the penthouse. I went back into my father's bedroom and found one of the hotel's maids in the bathroom. I learned afterwards that she shouldn't have been there, but she'd left her wedding ring in the bathroom when she had cleaned the penthouse earlier in the day, and she'd used her pass key to slip in and look for it. When I entered the penthouse, the maid hid because she thought she would be in trouble if I spotted her.'

'So did you help the maid to climb down the drainpipe?'

'No, she was too petrified to try. I couldn't even persuade her to leave the bathroom. I kept telling her we had to get out, but she was in acute shock and wouldn't move. We were both starting to choke because of the smoke and I knew we were going to die,' Nicolo said roughly.

'Then I had a brainwave. It was a long shot, but there was nothing else. I filled the bath with water and soaked a pile of towels which I draped over us before I dragged the maid through the blazing sitting room. The towels didn't cover my left side, and that's where I was burned the worst. I don't know *how* we made it to the door. I just remember the smoke and flames and the deafening roar of the furniture burning.'

'But you did make it,' Sophie said softly. 'If it hadn't been for your bravery the maid would have died. Maybe you did accidentally cause the fire, but your actions afterwards were heroic. Don't you see that?'

He laughed grimly. 'In the media's eyes I was a hero but that's because they didn't know the truth. Only my family knew what really happened. Naturally my father was furious. My brothers and sisters thought I had been stupid.'

Sometimes he wondered if his siblings would have been more sympathetic if he had told them he had proof their father had been unfaithful to their mother. But it had seemed a betrayal to speak of his mother's humiliation. He had guessed that his mother had found out about his father's infidelity, and that was why she had gone away. But Nicolo had been sure she would come back to the family and so he had never told anyone that he had seen Gene in bed with the chambermaid.

'Lucilla was kind,' he said gruffly. 'She, more than anyone else, took care of me. I owe her for that. But as I got older even Lucilla couldn't control me. I started drinking heavily to blank out the memories of what had happened. The media were fascinated by "the Chatsfield hero" as they labelled me. My private life became a running soap opera and there were plenty of women who were happy to take a starring role.'

His mouth curved cynically. 'You'd be amazed at the number of women who were curious to see my scars and treated it as a sick game to have sex with a monster.'

'Don't!' Sophie implored him, putting her hands over her ears to block out his bitter words. 'You're not a monster, and I can't believe any of those women thought you were. Why do you think so badly of yourself? You made one mistake when you were a boy. Are you going to punish yourself for the rest of your life?'

'Your compassion is a credit to you,' Nicolo said in an oddly strained tone. 'But perhaps you won't feel the same way when I tell you what happened to the chambermaid. Her life was ruined. As a result of smoke inhalation she developed a serious respiratory condition as well as panic attacks that left her unable to work. She was also badly burned, mainly on her face, and she was terribly disfigured.

'For many years after the fire I did not know what had happened to her. I was so wrapped up in myself that I did not even spare her a thought. But then I met her again— and the true horror of what I had done, the misery I had caused her, became apparent.'

He moved to stand by the window, watching the shadows lengthen as dusk fell. Nicolo did not know why he was telling Sophie details that he had never shared with anyone else, but as he spilled the poison that had festered inside him for so long he felt a sense of relief.

'One evening about eight years ago, the maid turned up at Chatsfield House. There was a party going on, and as usual I'd had too much to drink. When the butler told me a woman called Marissa Bisek wanted to see me I did not know who she was. After the fire I hadn't even bothered to find out her name.'

He sensed Sophie had come to stand next to him, but he did not look at her as he continued. 'I barely recognised Marissa. She looked as though she had aged thirty years, and one side of her face was scarred and misshapen. She told me that her husband had left her because he could not accept the way she looked, and because she was unable to work she was struggling to bring up her children on her own with very little money.'

He shook his head. 'For years she had read about my wild exploits in the newspapers. Nicolo Chatsfield—the playboy hero,' he mocked himself. 'And the worst thing was that Marissa *believed* I was a hero. She had no idea that *I* had started the fire, and *I* had ruined her life. I hadn't thought about her until she came to see me that night to beg for a little money to ease her dire financial situation.'

Nicolo glanced at Sophie, his eyes blazing with raw emotion. 'I was some hero, huh?'

'*Yes*, you were,' she said fiercely. 'If it hadn't been for your bravery, Marissa's children would not have grown up with their mother. Maybe Marissa's life was affected by the fire, but I'm sure she was grateful to you for saving her, and I'm sure she values her life all the more because she came close to losing it.'

Sophie could tell that Nicolo was puzzled by her passionate outburst. She had been left with long-term effects from cancer, but her life had been spared and for that she was utterly thankful.

'What happened to Marissa after she came to see you?'

'I took care of her and her children and arranged for the income I received from a family trust fund to be paid to Marissa instead of to me.' Nicolo exhaled heavily. 'I knew my life had to change. I despised the champagne-swilling womaniser I had become, and I hated the hero label that I did not deserve.'

Nicolo hesitated, wondering whether to tell Sophie about the charity that he had established. No one knew the identity of the mysterious benefactor who donated millions of pounds to the burns support foundation, and he preferred it that way.

'I took a long hard look at myself, and I did not like what I saw. I don't mean my scars,' he said as Sophie opened her mouth to speak. 'I didn't like the man inside here.' He touched his chest. 'I also realised that, having transferred the money to Marissa, I needed to work. Setting up my own hedge fund company seemed like a logical career decision.'

'And you quickly made a fortune,' Sophie commented. She understood that after all he had been through, Nicolo found it easier to live as a recluse and focus on the unemotional world of financial trading rather than interact with people. Yet she wondered if making all that money made him happy. She knew that he was still tormented by his past, and her heart ached for him.

Impulsively she took hold of his injured hand and ran her fingers gently over the ridges of scarred skin. Her emotions felt ragged and a lump formed in her throat.

'I wish you could forgive yourself,' she whispered.

Nicolo stiffened as he felt a tiny bead of moisture drop onto his scarred skin. He slid his other hand beneath Sophie's chin and tilted her head up.

'Tears, Sophie? Do you think they will heal my scars?'

She shook her head. 'Not your visible scars. And only you can heal the scars inside you. Nicolo—life is so precious,' she said urgently. 'I understand that better than most people.'

'*You?*' He gave a harsh laugh. 'I appreciate your sympathy, Sophie, but how can you possibly understand what it feels like to be in a situation where you believe you are going to die?'

'I understand because it happened to me too,' she said

fiercely. 'I don't mean that I was trapped in a fire, but I do know what it's like to face death.'

He frowned. 'What do you mean?'

Sophie took a deep breath. 'I had cancer when I was sixteen. I nearly died.'

Nicolo felt as if he had been kicked in the gut. Ordinarily he was quick to grasp facts. It was crucial for a financial trader to be able to think on his feet. But he was stunned by Sophie's revelation. She was so bright and brimming with life, it was impossible to imagine that she had once been ravaged by a life-threatening illness.

'What kind of cancer?' he asked roughly.

'Bone cancer—osteosarcoma is its proper name.' She sighed. 'It started when I developed a lump on my knee. I played a lot of tennis and thought I'd picked up an injury, but the lump got bigger, and when I went back to sixth form at school to start my A-levels I felt tired all the time and I couldn't shake off a cold. Eventually Mum insisted that I should see a doctor. She thought I might be lacking vitamins or there was some other simple explanation. A blood test revealed that I had an abnormal blood count and I was sent to the hospital for further tests.

'Within days the doctors discovered that the lump on my knee was an aggressive tumour and that the cancer had already spread to my pelvis. That was the beginning of months of chemo. At one point it looked as though I might have to have my leg amputated, which was pretty grim.' Sophie tried to keep her tone light and was unaware of the tremor in her voice as she spoke of the darkest days of her illness.

Watching the emotions flit across her features, Nicolo felt an overwhelming desire to pull her into his arms and hold her close, but she was speaking again, and he sensed she felt a need to talk about what had happened to her.

'It was a difficult time, not only for me, but for my parents. My mother cut down on her legal work so that she could be with me while I was in hospital.' She bit her lip. 'I was a teenage girl, and the thing that upset me the most was when my hair fell out as a result of the chemotherapy. But I was lucky, the treatment worked and I was finally given the all-clear two years later. I was able to go to university and get on with my life, but I'll always be grateful that I was given a second chance and I am determined to make the most of every day of my life.'

She stared at Nicolo. 'I know you suffered terrible injuries in the fire, but your life was spared, and I wish you could seize every day, every moment.'

He was silent, and when he finally spoke his voice shook with a strange intensity, as if it had been wrenched from his soul. 'Do you?'

Sophie's eyes flew to his, and her heart missed a beat when she saw desire glittering in his gaze. Instantly she felt a fierce hunger rip through her body, a need so great that it made her bones ache and her blood pound through her veins. The air between them trembled with raw emotion.

Nicolo was still reeling from what Sophie had told him. Like him, she had faced her own mortality when she had been little more than a child. It explained her compassionate nature, he mused, feeling a strong wave of admiration for her. The fact that Sophie had survived her terrifying ordeal was, he was sure, due in no small part to her sheer determination not to let cancer beat her. He felt a connection to her on a deeply personal level and he was ashamed that he had scorned her cheerfulness. Certainly he understood her mantra to 'live for the moment.'

'What would you say if I told you that I'm desperate to

seize *this* moment, and make love to you as I have wanted to do since the day you arrived here?' he said roughly.

Sophie's heart missed a beat when she saw the feral gleam in Nicolo's eyes. It was as if they had both laid bare their emotions, and she felt vulnerable and yet excited by the sexual chemistry fizzing between them.

'You threw me out of the house,' she reminded him shakily.

'Because I recognised the threat you posed to my sanity.'

Nicolo swore savagely and pulled her hard against his chest. 'I'm no good for you,' he growled. 'But God forgive me, I can't fight this any longer. I have to have you, Sophie.'

When he had caught sight of her walking across the garden, an ethereal figure in her silvery-grey silk dress and her golden hair rippling in the breeze, he had known that the battle was over. He could not deny his desire for her, especially now he knew that she had almost lost her life to cancer. Life was frighteningly fragile, and he was thankful that her life had been spared.

Sophie was not like the countless women he had taken to bed during the years when he had been a playboy. He looked back on his behaviour with shame and had vowed never to have casual sex again. But Sophie was different. She evoked an emotional response in him that he had never felt before. Right now Nicolo was not ready to define exactly what he was feeling. All he knew was that Sophie had crept beneath his defences. He threaded his fingers into her long honey-blonde hair, capturing her while he brought his head down and kissed her mouth as if he had been starving for a long, long time, and she was his salvation.

Sophie could not have resisted even if she had wanted

to. The moment Nicolo's lips claimed hers she surrendered to the wildfire passion which exploded between them. His mouth moved with firm demand over hers, tasting her, taking her unguarded response and building her desire as he boldly pushed his tongue between her lips. Her brain registered that this was madness, but her body did not heed the warning. Molten heat pooled between her thighs as he moved his hands restlessly over her, tracing the shape of her hips and breasts.

When he lifted her into his arms she linked her hands around his neck and kissed him with such sweet intensity that he gave a harsh groan and strode out of the room and up the stairs, heading towards his bedroom with a purposeful intent that made Sophie tremble with anticipation.

The room was shadowed with the soft purple darkness of night newly arrived. Through the open window Sophie heard a blackbird singing its last song of the dying day, but she barely registered the sweet serenade, for her whole being was attuned to Nicolo. She heard the swift, ragged sound of his breathing mingled with her own shallow breaths, the soft slither of silk as he unzipped her dress and it fell to the floor. Her heart thudded as he laid her on the bed and knelt over her, his hands deftly removing her bra while he kissed her mouth, her throat, pressing lower until he flicked his tongue across one of her nipples and she gave a soft cry of delight.

The ache low in her pelvis was growing ever more insistent. The exquisite sensation of Nicolo suckling each of her nipples in turn fuelled Sophie's impatience to take the hard length of his arousal deep inside her. She lifted her hands and undid the buttons on his shirt before sliding it from him. In the darkened room she could not see his face clearly and could only make out the shape of his formidable shoulders and broad chest.

She reached out her hand and found the switch on the bedside lamp.

Nicolo stiffened as they were both illuminated in the lamplight.

'Turn the light off,' he said roughly. 'I'm sure you don't want to see my disfigured body. I could leave my shirt on if you wish?'

Sophie heard the vulnerability in his voice that he could not quite disguise, and her heart turned over. She deliberately ran her hands over the mottled skin covering his arm and one side of his chest.

'I've seen your scars before and I didn't pass out in horror,' she said strongly. 'They don't make any difference to the way I feel.' Cupping his face in her hands, she looked steadily into his eyes. 'You're the sexiest man I've ever met and I've never been so turned on as I am right now. I want to watch you make love to me,' she said huskily.

'*Sweet Jesus*, Sophie…' Nicolo's throat moved convulsively. He felt unbearably moved by her words and by the honesty blazing in her eyes. Her insistence that she was excited by the thought of watching him make love to her healed the wounds inside him that had hurt far more than his physical injuries.

He moved his eyes down her body and a fierce, almost barbaric need to possess her swept through him. She was so beautiful. He traced his hands over the satiny skin of her shoulders, down to her firm, rounded breasts with their dusky pink nipples jutting provocatively, inviting him to caress them. He loved the little whimpers she made when he kissed her breasts, loved that she was so responsive to his touch.

He trailed his fingers lightly over her stomach, moving inexorably lower to discover the silky skin of her inner thighs. He was shaking with the force of his desire, but an unwelcome thought pushed into his brain and he could not ignore it. Cursing beneath his breath he snatched his hand from her body.

Sophie was confused as she stared at Nicolo's tense expression. She wondered why he had stopped. Her stomach swooped as she remembered how he had rejected her in the walled garden, and her insecurities returned with a vengeance. Maybe she did not turn him on? Why else would the glittering desire in his eyes have faded?

'What's wrong?' she whispered, trembling with tension. If he rejected her for a second time, she did not think she could bear it.

He gave her a rueful look. 'I don't have any protection. I'm sorry, angel, but I'm sure neither of us wants to risk an unplanned pregnancy.'

'Oh,' Sophie murmured as comprehension finally dawned. Relief swept through her that the reason Nicolo had halted making love to her was not because he did not desire her. The hard, hungry kiss he dropped on her mouth proved quite the opposite, as did the hard ridge of his arousal she could feel pressing against her thigh.

'I don't believe it.' He groaned as he rolled onto his back. He caught hold of her hand and brought it to his mouth, kissing her fingers with an unexpected tenderness that swirled around Sophie's heart. 'The chemist in the village is shut, but there's a garage on the main road that might sell condoms. I could be there and back in fifteen minutes, if you'll wait that long.' A tremor ran through his aroused body. 'I'm not sure I can,' he said with feeling.

Sophie took pity on him. 'You don't have to wait, or drive to find an all-night chemist. The fact is—' she swallowed '—the fact is there's no risk of me falling pregnant. The chemotherapy left me infertile.'

Nicolo felt a curious little tug in his chest. He lifted his hand and brushed her hair back from her face. 'That must have been pretty devastating news.'

'To be honest, having survived cancer, being told that I'd probably never have children didn't seem like the end of the world. I was just glad to be alive.'

Once again Nicolo felt admiration for Sophie's optimism and her refusal to feel sorry for herself. 'You're amazing,' he murmured softly as he drew her face down to his and claimed her mouth in a kiss that quickly became intensely erotic. He recalled how she had said that he turned her on, but he had not even begun yet and he resolved to give her the most pleasurable experience of her life.

With her doubts allayed, Sophie relaxed against the pillows and curled her arms around Nicolo's neck as he continued to kiss her mouth, her throat and her breasts. She could not control the tremors that shook her body as he stroked his fingertips across her stomach and then moved lower, brushing lightly over the strip of silk between her legs. Desire tugged low in her pelvis. When he pulled her knickers down she lifted her hips to aid him and released her breath on a ragged sigh when he pushed her thighs apart.

She was glad she had insisted on leaving the lamp on when she saw dull colour flare along his cheekbones as he looked at her. She could feel moist warmth between her legs and knew he must be able to see the evidence of her arousal.

Wantonly she spread her legs wider and heard him give a feral groan that increased her excitement to a feverish need. She caught her breath as he gently parted her and probed her eager flesh with one finger and then two, pushing deep into her and exploring her with a devastating efficiency that turned her bones to liquid.

She was ready for him, and her disappointment when he withdrew his fingers was mingled with relief that he must surely now intend to make love to her fully. But instead of positioning himself ready to take her, he bent his head and she felt his breath stir the narrow strip of golden curls that hid her feminine heart as he bestowed a shockingly intimate caress.

Sweet heaven! Sophie arched her hips involuntarily, seeking even greater pleasure from his sensual foreplay. She felt her internal muscles tighten, and she gasped, gripping his shoulders as she fought the first spasms of her orgasm. What he was doing to her with his tongue was good, unbelievably good, but her body demanded more and was desperate for his ultimate possession.

Nicolo sensed her frustration and was aware that his own need was building to a fierce urgency that could only have one conclusion. He made a raw sound deep in his throat as he felt Sophie's fingers curl around his swollen shaft, and when she began to move her hand rhythmically his jaw clenched as he sought to control the hot tide of desire that threatened to overwhelm him.

He pulled her hand away and gave her a wry smile. 'Not this time, angel, or this could be over embarrassingly quickly.'

Once again the faint vulnerability in his voice tugged on Sophie's heart. But when she looked at him the hungry glitter in his gaze caused her stomach muscles to tighten. His eyes held hers as he lifted himself over her and pressed forward so that the tip of his erection rubbed against her moist opening. She felt a brief flare of doubt when she realised just how big he was, but her eager body was receptive and when he thrust into her she gasped with pleasure as he filled her.

Dimly the thought came to her that this was what she had been made for, with this man. Her highwayman demanded her complete capitulation and she gave herself to him willingly and allowed him to plunder her body with his powerful strokes, each thrust more intense than the last.

Her passion matched his and she lifted her hips to urge him on, to thrust deeper, harder, faster, hurtling them both towards an ecstasy that could only belong to two bodies moving in total accord and two souls linked inescapably.

Sophie could feel herself slipping into a state where conscious thought was obliterated by exquisite sensation. Nicolo's driving rhythm dominated her mind and her body and she gave a choked cry as the first ripples of her climax caused her internal muscles to clench and unclench in tremulous undulations.

She was near, so near. Keeping her eyes wide open, she watched him making love to her and felt a fierce tenderness for this scarred, enigmatic man who was haunted by his past.

'Let go,' she whispered against his lips. He stiffened, his big body shaking with tension as he stared down at her, and then he drove into her with a shockingly powerful thrust that made Sophie cry out as her body splintered and she was swept up in a rapturous orgasm. The tremors shuddering through her came in wave after wave, and in their midst she heard Nicolo give a hoarse groan as he reached his own nirvana and spilled into her.

CHAPTER NINE

Dawn was a long time coming. It seemed to Nicolo that a lifetime had passed before the stars outside the window went out one by one and the sky slowly lightened. He knew he should get out of bed. His reluctance to move away from Sophie's warm body was a stark reminder of his stupidity, yet it took all of his willpower to slide out from beneath the sheet.

He did not remember falling asleep last night. If he had been thinking straight he would have got up immediately after they'd had sex. But clearly his brain had not been functioning, he thought derisively. If it had, he would not have slept with Sophie, and he would not now be trying to extricate himself from her arm that she had looped around his waist, and from a situation that he should not have allowed to happen.

He pulled on his robe, but instead of heading for the bathroom and a cold shower, he stared down at her rose-flushed face and her honey-gold hair spread across the pillows and his gut twisted. She was so very lovely—inside and out. Sophie's beauty was not superficial; it went to her very core. It was hard to believe that he had found her bright and cheerful nature irritating when she had first arrived.

It would have been better for both their sakes if she

had driven away from Chatsfield House and not returned, he thought grimly. When he had woken sometime after midnight and found her curled up against him he had sensed he was in trouble. For all Sophie's assertion that she believed in seizing the moment, he had a feeling that even while she was sleeping she was making plans for their relationship which involved expectations he could not fulfil.

He had too much baggage. He was too screwed up by his past to be able to offer any woman a relationship. Eight years ago, when he had given up his wild, womanising ways and turned his life onto a different track, he'd had to face the fact that his selfish behaviour had hurt a lot of people. He did not intend to risk hurting anyone else. His work for the burns support charity was his focus now. Becoming involved with Sophie would be a distraction he neither wanted nor needed.

Sophie knew where she was before she had opened her eyes. As she stirred awake she instantly recalled the previous night that she had spent with Nicolo, and a sense of well-being swept through her when she remembered his unexpected tenderness as he had made love to her.

She supposed she should not be surprised. Sexual awareness had simmered between them from the moment he had accused her of trespassing on his property. Last night it had exploded in a firestorm of passion that brought a rueful smile to her lips as she thought of her ardent response to him.

She was twenty-six, she reminded herself. Too old to blush like a schoolgirl as memories of Nicolo kissing *every* part of her body filled her mind. Maybe the next time they made love she would gift him the same pleasure.

Shocked by the erotic images inside her head, she

lifted her lashes and discovered that she was alone in the bed. She immediately saw Nicolo standing by the window, dressed in his customary black jeans and leather boots and a loose-fitting white silk shirt. She was disappointed that she had not woken in his arms. Remembering the sensual pleasures they had shared last night caused molten heat to pool between her thighs, and she longed for him to come back to bed and make love to her again. But something about his rigid stance sent a prickle of unease through Sophie.

'Good morning.'

He swung round at the sound of her voice but did not return the greeting or her tentative smile. The early morning sunlight threw his chiselled features into sharp relief. His face looked as though it had been carved from granite, Sophie thought, feeling chilled by the hard gleam in his eyes.

'I've made you some tea,' he said unexpectedly.

As he walked towards the bed she noticed a tray bearing a teapot and cup and saucer on the bedside table. She should have been touched by his thoughtful gesture, but her instincts were telling her that behind his calm facade Nicolo was incredibly tense.

'Shall I pour you a cup?' he said abruptly.

'In a minute.' She forced the words past the lump that had formed in her throat. She did not understand why the tender lover of last night had disappeared and been replaced with a remote stranger. Glancing at the clock, she was shocked to see that it was nearly ten o'clock. She had never slept in so late in her life, but it wasn't surprising after the energetic night she had spent making love with Nicolo, she thought ruefully.

'I must get up,' she muttered. Unthinkingly she threw back the sheet and tensed as she remembered she was naked. Colour flared in her cheeks as she glanced down at her body and saw its treacherous response to Nicolo, her nipples immediately hardening in provocative invitation.

She could not prevent her eyes from darting to him and she drew a swift breath when she glimpsed a look of raw, possessive hunger in his eyes before his lashes swept down and his expression became hooded. It should have helped to know that he still wanted her, but it was beginning to dawn on her that while for her last night had been a magical and emotive experience, for Nicolo it had just been sex.

He watched dispassionately as she hauled the sheet up to her chin.

'I've decided to attend the shareholders' meeting.'

'Oh!' She stared at him, nonplussed by his announcement. 'That's good to hear. I'm sure you won't regret your decision.'

'That remains to be seen,' he said sardonically. 'It means, of course, that you will no longer need to stay at Chatsfield House. You said you would return to London once you had gained my agreement,' he reminded her.

A dull weight settled in Sophie's chest. Clearly he was impatient to get rid of her. 'Nicolo, what's wrong?' she said in a low voice. 'Why are you doing this?'

He swung away from the bed, and she had the impression that he wanted to avoid her gaze.

'Last night was fun,' he said coolly, 'but to spend a second night together would be foolish.' When Sophie did not reply, he said in a deeper tone, 'When you've had time to think about it, I'm certain you will agree with me.'

She was tempted to argue, to remind him that what they had shared last night had been special. But perhaps it hadn't been special to him, she thought sickly. When he had held her in his arms in the sweet aftermath of their physical union she could have sworn that he had felt, as she had, a connection between them that defied explanation.

She must have read the signs wrong, she told herself. She had done the same thing with Richard when she had believed that he loved her. *Stupid Sophie*, would she ever learn that men were not to be trusted? She had loved three men in her life, but her father, Richard and now Nicolo had let her down. Her heart jolted. She wasn't in love with Nicolo, she assured herself. Then why did she feel so betrayed and bereft by his rejection? whispered a little voice in her head.

Pride brought Sophie's head up and her voice was steady as she said, 'You're right, of course. Christos needs me back at the office, and as you say, there's no reason for me to prolong my visit. I'll leave as soon as I've packed.'

No way, she told herself fiercely, would she beg him to let her stay. She did not understand why her heart was urging her to fight for a relationship with Nicolo. It was never going to be easy to break down his barriers, her heart argued, but unless she tried she would never know if there was a chance for them.

Don't be a fool, her brain retaliated. Why would she even want a relationship with a man who was so damaged by his past that he had cut himself off from the world and even refused to have anything to do with his father and his family's hotel business?

She glanced at his stern profile and felt a flare of pain—a mixture of anger, hurt and frustration—that she could not dent the armour plating surrounding his heart.

'I feel sorry for you,' she said huskily. 'Not because of your scars,' she continued quickly when he frowned, 'but for the fact that you can't or won't forgive yourself for causing the fire all those years ago. No one can change the past, and life moves on. You were given a second chance, but instead of making the most of your life you hide away in this house feeling sorry for yourself.

'It's the truth,' she cried as Nicolo's eyes blazed with anger. 'You made one mistake twenty years ago and you've punished yourself ever since. Your life is worth more than that, Nicolo. You've achieved a lot, but you could achieve so much more. I don't believe that your father and brothers and sisters still blame you for what happened when you were a boy. But if you want them to be proud of you, and if you want to feel proud of yourself, you have to stop blaming yourself.'

Sophie made it sound so easy, Nicolo thought bitterly. But she did not have to live with the knowledge that her actions had ruined another person's life. It was true that he had helped Marissa Bisek since he had discovered how she had suffered after the fire, but the money he gave her felt like blood money to assuage his guilt.

He looked over at Sophie. She had pulled the sheet tightly round her, but rather than disguise her body, the material moulded her soft curves and outlined the firm mounds of her breasts. He had a flashback to the previous night when he had traced his hands over her warm, naked flesh and suckled her pebble-hard nipples until she had moaned with pleasure.

Dio! He resented his body's urgent response to her, and resented the inexplicable hold she had over him. It was just sexual, he told himself. Deep down he feared the truth was more complicated.

His jaw clenched. 'Are you done with the amateur psychoanalysis?' He glanced at his watch. 'I have work to do,' he growled, and strode out of the room before he gave in to the damnable craving to rip the sheet away and take possession of her slender body.

* * *

The email arrived in Nicolo's inbox just before five-thirty in the afternoon. Usually he did not read emails until he'd finished working for the day, but the name of the sender caught his attention. It was five weeks since Sophie had driven away from Chatsfield House and there had been no communication between them during that time. He could not deny he was curious to know why she was contacting him now.

The message was brief and to the point.

Christos Giatrakos has had to go abroad at short notice and therefore tomorrow's shareholders' meeting has been postponed until his return.
S. Ashdown.

He read the email twice, wondering why he felt disappointed. She had not even signed off as Sophie, Nicolo noticed as he stared at the impersonal S. Ashdown. They had spent a night of incredible passion together, but she hadn't bothered to use her name. Anger burned in his gut. The dismissive tone of the email indicated that the night they had made love had meant nothing to her. No doubt she had not thought about him since she had returned to London, while he had found himself thinking about her too often for his liking.

And now that the shareholders' meeting had been cancelled he had no excuse to go to London and see her again. He swung round in his chair and stared out of the window at the rain hammering against the panes. Dorcha got up from the rug where he had been sprawled and padded over to lay his shaggy head on Nicolo's knee.

The wolfhound whined, and Nicolo sighed heavily. 'Okay, I admit it. I miss her.' He stroked Dorcha's ears.

'So, what am I supposed to do? Have you got any suggestions?' He found no answers in the dog's soulful eyes and muttering a curse he turned back to the bank of computer monitors that were flashing numbers at him.

Sophie leaned over the sink and splashed cold water onto her face. The bout of sickness had left her feeling weak and drained. Glancing in the mirror, she grimaced at her sallow complexion. She wouldn't look out of place in a waxworks museum, she thought grimly. Thankfully she was in a private cloakroom that was only used by the office staff of the Chatsfield London. At least there was no danger that any of the hotel's glamorous clientele would have heard her losing the contents of her stomach.

Christos had commented before he had left for Greece that she looked awful. 'While I'm away I want you to see a doctor,' he'd instructed. 'I know you said you're suffering from a gastric virus, but it shouldn't last this long. Maybe something more serious is wrong with you.'

She had laughed off Christos's concern, but she *was* worried about her health, Sophie acknowledged. At first she had blamed her excessive tiredness on the fact that she had felt utterly miserable since Nicolo had sent her away from Chatsfield House, and she had assumed that her mood swings and lack of appetite were for the same reason. But over the past couple of weeks she had started to feel nauseous, and she had actually vomited several times. It brought back memories of when she had been sixteen and had kept on being sick. 'I'm taking you to see Dr Williams,' her mother had insisted. '*Something* is the matter with you.'

Her mother's instincts had proved right, Sophie brooded. But surely her cancer could not have come back? She had checked her body for strange lumps and found nothing, but her common sense told her that she needed to visit her GP to find out why she felt unwell.

She walked back to her office and glanced at the clock. It was only 4:00 p.m. The day had dragged and she knew it was because she was disappointed not to have seen Nicolo. She was an idiot to have psyched herself up to meet him again. After all, he had made it plain that one night of sex was all he had wanted.

Her head ached, and she could not concentrate on the report she was supposed to be amending. Coming to a decision, she went into the adjoining office and spoke to Lucilla's assistant. 'Jessie, can you take Christos's calls for the rest of the afternoon? I'm going home early.'

'Yes, of course,' Jessie said sympathetically. 'I've noticed that you've looked pale for a few days now. Maybe you should see a doctor?'

Sophie nodded. 'I'll make an appointment with my GP when I get home.'

Back at her flat, she lay down on the bed, intending to take a short nap, and woke hours later feeling ravenous. She reheated the casserole that she hadn't fancied the previous day and felt a lot better after she'd eaten.

The trouble with sleeping in the day was that now she was wide awake, and she ran a bath, hoping that a long soak in a fragrant bubble bath would help her to relax. It was dark outside by the time she pulled the plug and smoothed body lotion over her skin before wrapping herself in a fluffy towelling bathrobe. The ring of the doorbell was unexpected at this time of night and she put the safety chain in place before she opened the door.

'Nicolo!' Shock strangled her vocal chords so that her voice emerged as a tremulous whisper.

He was leaning nonchalantly against the door frame, his arms folded across his chest. Dressed in a pale grey suit and a black silk shirt, with the top buttons undone, a grey tie hanging loose down his front and his dark hair falling over his collar, he looked so incredibly sexy that Sophie's breath became trapped in her lungs.

Clutching the edge of the door for support, she dredged up her pride and managed to sound coolly uninterested. 'What are you doing here?' A thought struck her. 'You did receive my email telling you that the shareholders' meeting was cancelled, didn't you?'

Nicolo was tempted to deny it, but while he was debating what to say Sophie must have assumed from his silence that he had not got her message.

He shrugged. 'Now that I'm here, are you going to invite me in?'

He had a nerve when she hadn't heard a word from him in five weeks. 'Why?' she demanded bluntly.

His reply was unexpected. 'We need to talk.'

Her heart gave a jolt. She had every right to tell him to go to hell, Sophie reminded herself, but her fingers were already fumbling to release the safety chain so that she could open the door.

He stepped into the narrow hall and she immediately felt swamped by his potent masculinity. He was too tall, too big, too overwhelming, she thought as she led the way into the small living room. She was regretting allowing him into her home. She would give him five minutes to say what he wanted to say, and then she would ask him to leave.

Nicolo glanced around at the pale lemon walls and cream sofa. A glass-topped dining table and two chairs stood in front of the window. The television in one corner was the only other item of furniture. A door leading off the room led to a tiny kitchen.

'Nice place,' he murmured in an attempt to break the prickling tension. 'It's…compact.'

She watched Nicolo prowling around the tiny sitting room like a caged tiger and her tension escalated. It was too much to bear to be standing so close to him when a great chasm divided them, and she searched for an excuse to leave the room while she tried to regain her composure.

'Would you like some coffee?' she said stiffly.

His eyes rested on her flushed cheeks, his expression indecipherable. Had he expected a more enthusiastic greeting? she wondered. Why should he after he'd made it plain that he wasn't interested in a relationship with her?

'Why not?' he drawled. 'Coffee sounds good.'

Who was he kidding? Nicolo asked himself derisively as he followed Sophie into the kitchen that was barely bigger than a cupboard. Ever since he had watched her walk out of Chatsfield House and get into her car without once glancing back, he had done his damnedest to forget her—and failed. Her image seemed to be burned onto his retinas, and her last words to him had lingered in his mind.

Sophie had told him that he needed to forgive himself for the things he had done in his past. But his guilt about Marissa Bisek tortured his soul. That was why he had sent Sophie away. He could not be the sort of man she deserved and he could not contemplate the kind of meaningful relationship with her that he suspected she would like. Five weeks ago he had decided that it would not be right to have an affair with her, but standing close to her in the miniscule kitchen it was hard to remember his good intentions.

His memory had not done her justice, he thought ruefully. She looked stunning. Her skin was almost luminescent and her hazel eyes shone with a fierce brilliance. He dropped his gaze to the edges of her bathrobe that gaped slightly, revealing the creamy upper slopes of her breasts.

It suddenly occurred to Nicolo that she was naked beneath the robe and his body throbbed with an urgency that made him catch his breath.

Sophie fussed about, filling the kettle and taking the coffee and sugar jars from a cupboard. She was conscious of Nicolo's intense scrutiny and her nerves felt as taut as an overstretched elastic band. She finished making two mugs of instant coffee and was hit by a wave of nausea. It reminded her of her fears about her health, but she had no intention of revealing her concerns to Nicolo. She turned to face him, crossing her arms in front of her in an unconsciously defensive gesture.

'So what do you want to talk about that's so important it couldn't wait until a more reasonable hour?' she asked tersely. 'It's ten o'clock,' she pointed out when his brows lifted. 'I want to go to bed.'

The moment the words left her mouth she realised how suggestive they sounded and she flushed hotly.

'Actually,' Nicolo murmured in a voice as seductive as molten syrup, 'I've changed my mind.'

His gaze lingered on the front of her robe and Sophie felt her breasts swell. The friction of her hard nipples rubbing against the towelling robe was shockingly erotic and the bold gleam in Nicolo's eyes made her heart pound.

'You mean you don't want coffee?' she choked.

'No.' He reached out and gripped the lapels of her robe. In slow motion, it seemed, he pulled her towards him. 'I don't want coffee,' he said softly, 'I want you.'

Of course she was going to tell him to get lost. Angry colour flared on Sophie's cheeks. Did he really think he could walk into her flat and she would drop her knickers, just because he fancied sex rather than coffee?

She wasn't wearing any knickers; the thought slid into her head and molten heat flowed through her veins. She felt furious and vulnerable and, oh, God, *so* turned on. Her eyes widened as he lowered his head. She still could not quite believe that he was here, that he was going to...

A tremor shook her as Nicolo brushed his mouth across hers. One touch was all it took, Sophie thought despairingly as her lips parted of their own accord and a shaft of piercing need arrowed down to her pelvis.

'Sophie...' He growled her name, his voice raw with sexual hunger. And then his mouth was on hers once more, forceful, demanding a response she could not deny him or herself.

For the first time in five weeks the heavy weight in her heart lifted and she felt alive again, every nerve ending on her body quivering with anticipation as he pulled her against his muscular frame and wrapped his arms around her. When he lifted her up a voice inside her head warned that she must resist him, anything else would be madness. But as she turned her face into the tanned column of his throat and breathed in the scent of him—masculine, sensual and utterly addictive—her breath left her body in a shuddering sigh and the fight went out of her.

It was not difficult to locate her bedroom in the small flat. As he shouldered the door Nicolo had a vague impression of a pretty, feminine room and his shadow of doubt that maybe there was some other guy in her life disappeared. His instincts had told him that Sophie did not have casual affairs. She was a one-man kind of woman, but rather than sending him running, the thought filled him with an unexpected sense of satisfaction.

Her skin was satin-soft beneath his lips as he trailed his mouth down her throat while he deftly untied the belt of her robe. He pushed the bathrobe over her shoulders and groaned as he freed her breasts and they spilled into his hands. Her nipples were as hard as pebbles and he remembered how much she had enjoyed him touching them as he rolled the taut peaks between his fingers, gently, and then not so gently, and felt desire corkscrew through him when she moaned softly.

Urgency overwhelmed him. In all his womanising years he had never felt this level of hunger. Sophie aroused a primitive need in him to claim his woman and possess her utterly. With shaking hands he pulled off his jacket and shirt. The light emitted from the bedside lamps revealed the full horror of his scars, but he did not feel the need to hide them because he knew that Sophie did not care about his disfigurement. When he looked into her eyes he saw only desire and he brought his mouth down on hers again in a kiss that quickly deepened and became intensely erotic.

'Nicolo,' she whispered softly, pleadingly, as he pushed her legs apart and ran his fingertips up and down her moist opening. She arched her hips, her body quivering, eager, as he dipped into her honeyed sweetness and swirled his fingers in a rhythmic dance until she gasped and clutched his shoulders, urging him down onto her.

He was out of control, his erection pushing between her thighs, straining to sink into the velvet embrace of her body.

'What are you doing to me?' he muttered. And then he thrust into her, deep and hard, driving the breath from her as he filled her.

He stilled, shaken by the intensity of his desire. 'Did I hurt you?'

'No. Don't stop.' Sophie delivered the words like a burst of gunfire. She could hardly speak or think as the sensation of Nicolo's swollen length pulsing inside her, pushing deeper, sent her spiralling out of control. She was glad he wasn't gentle, and gloried in his sensual mastery.

He was so big and powerful, poised above her. He moved again, taking her with steady strokes, his pace increasing as she arched her hips to accept every powerful thrust. Her body belonged to him, Sophie acknowledged. And moments later, as they simultaneously reached a shattering climax, the terrifying thought slipped into her mind that so did her heart.

CHAPTER TEN

OH, YOU FOOL, was Sophie's first thought when she opened her eyes early the next morning and saw Nicolo's head on the pillow beside her. The standard-size double bed was too small for his big frame, and she was supremely conscious of his naked body pressed up close against her. The weight of his hair-roughened thigh slung across her hips and the languorous ache in her muscles were stark reminders that she had not dreamed they had made love last night. Now, in the cold light of day, she was mortified that she had not even attempted to resist him. He'd only had to click his fingers and she had fallen into bed with him.

She studied his face. His features were softer in sleep, his mouth less stern. His thick black lashes fanned his cheeks and his olive skin was a testament to his Italian heritage. He looked exotic and sexy and Sophie felt a delicious coiling sensation in the pit of her stomach as she thought of him easing his powerful erection into her.

Enough, she told herself disgustedly. She was not going to lie here like a concubine waiting for her master to wake and take his pleasure with her. She jerked upright and swung her legs over the side of the bed. Her stomach churned and, grabbing her robe, she raced into the en suite bathroom with barely enough time to close the door before she was sick.

When she walked back into the bedroom ten minutes later, Nicolo was sitting up in bed with a pillow propped behind his head and the sheet draped low over his hips. He studied her pale face, his eyes questioning. Sophie looked away from him and walked across the room to stand by the window, watching a road sweeper pushing his broom over the cobblestones in Covent Garden.

'What's going on?' he said quietly. 'I spoke to a woman at your office called Jessie, and she told me you've been suffering from a gastric upset for a few weeks. She also said she thinks you're not eating properly.'

Sophie flushed. 'I can't believe you discussed personal details about me with a member of the office staff.'

Nicolo ignored her outburst. 'I noticed last night that you have lost weight. And you seem different, more subdued.' Was the change in her his fault? he wondered grimly. He knew he had hurt her feelings when he had sent her away from Chatsfield House. *This* was why he steered clear of relationships, Nicolo thought bitterly. He had known he was no good for her, and her tangible unhappiness increased his sense of guilt.

She hesitated. 'It's true that I have been feeling unwell lately. It's probably nothing….' A feeling of dread settled like concrete in the pit of her stomach and suddenly she could not keep her fears to herself. 'My symptoms are similar to when I was ill when I was sixteen,' she blurted out. She hugged her arms around herself as she turned to face Nicolo. 'I'm worried that the cancer has come back.'

Nicolo stared at her, too shocked for a few seconds to speak. *Santa Madre*, no! Don't let it be true, a voice inside him shouted. The fearful expression on Sophie's face made him bury his own fear and he asked calmly, 'Have you seen a doctor?'

'I've got an appointment at the end of the week. The surgery is very busy,' Sophie explained.

'That's no damned good. You can't wait another three days.' Nicolo leapt out of bed, pulled on his trousers and grabbed his mobile phone. 'You need to see a specialist today.'

'I don't want to make a fuss.'

Nicolo cast Sophie a look she could not define, but she felt a sense of relief that he was taking charge. 'You might not want to, angel, but I'm prepared to make the biggest fuss imaginable to find out what's wrong with you. I have a friend in Harley Street. Hugh is a fantastic doctor, and I can guarantee he'll fit you into his morning's appointments.'

An hour later, Sophie felt a fraud as she was ushered into Dr Hugh Bryant's plush office that was a million miles away from the sterile and faintly depressing hospital wards where she had spent so much time as a teenager.

'I feel bad for making a fuss over what is probably nothing, Dr Bryant,' she murmured.

'Call me Hugh,' he said with a smile. 'Nicolo explained on the phone that you have been experiencing extreme tiredness and nausea for a few weeks. He also said that you were successfully treated for cancer about ten years ago.'

'Yes.' She shot a glance at Nicolo, who was sitting beside her. She had been surprised when he had accompanied her into the doctor's office, but she was touched by his show of support.

She gave the doctor a brief explanation of how she had developed osteosarcoma when she had been sixteen, and mentioned that the massive doses of chemotherapy she had received to fight the disease had left her infertile.

'Ordinarily I would suggest that your symptoms could be an indication of pregnancy,' Hugh told her. 'But obviously in your case it seems unlikely that you might have conceived. And of course pregnancy would be impossible if you haven't had unprotected sex.' Catching Sophie's expression he murmured, 'It would be an idea to do a pregnancy test so that we can rule it out completely.'

She shrugged. 'All right, but I'm certain the result will be negative. I had some tests a couple of years ago which showed that I wasn't ovulating.'

Sophie went into another room with a nurse to give a sample before returning to the doctor's office where Hugh asked her some more questions about her general health. He paused to answer his phone, and his expression was serious when he ended the brief call.

Sophie felt a frisson of fear. The nurse had also taken a blood sample to see if she was anaemic. She remembered that she had been found to have a low red blood cell count when her cancer had been diagnosed. Could there be a problem with her blood count? The idea made her feel sick with terror as memories of how wretched the chemotherapy had made her feel came flooding back. There had been a few occasions during her months of treatment when she had almost given up her fight for life. Now she wondered if she was mentally strong enough to battle cancer for a second time.

Hugh Bryant gave a wry smile. 'You should both be prepared for a shock,' he said gently.

'What do you mean?' Nicolo demanded in a tense voice. To Sophie's surprise he reached out and clasped her hand. His fingers were warm and strong, and she was grateful for his strength as Hugh spoke again.

'The pregnancy test is positive.'

For a few seconds the world tilted on its axis. The

words made no sense. Sophie had mentally prepared herself for the likelihood that she would need further tests to see if she had cancer. It had not occurred to her that she might actually be pregnant.

'It's not possible,' she said sharply at the same time as she heard Nicolo's swiftly indrawn breath. 'I was told that the chemotherapy had damaged my fertility and I would be unable to have children.'

'It is not unheard of for women who stopped ovulating as a result of chemotherapy to resume ovulation several years later,' Hugh explained. He smiled. 'One thing I've learned during my medical career is that sometimes miracles happen.

'Obviously the pregnancy is unplanned, and I expect you will both need some time to come to terms with what has happened,' he said quietly. 'Nicolo, I suggest you take Sophie home so that she can rest. You are clearly both in a state of shock.'

Shock! Nicolo almost laughed at the understatement. He felt as if his lungs were being crushed in a vice and every last atom of oxygen was being squeezed out of his body. He glanced at Sophie's white face and feared she was going to faint. It was obvious that she had believed she was unable to conceive. He should not have taken a risk, and should have waited until he had bought contraceptives before he'd had sex with her, he berated himself. But it was too late for blame now that Sophie was expecting his child.

Trapped in a haze of numb disbelief, Sophie was barely aware of Nicolo guiding her out of the doctor's office and out to the car. They were both silent on the journey back to her flat, and once inside she automatically walked into the kitchen and put the kettle on.

'Let me do that,' Nicolo insisted. 'I expect you want a cup of tea?'

'No, I seem to have gone off tea....' She blanched as the reason for her change in tastes suddenly made sense. Some of her friends had complained that they had disliked tea and coffee in the early months of pregnancy. 'I'd like some warm blackcurrant cordial,' she said dully.

A few minutes later Nicolo set down a tray with their drinks on the dining table and glanced at Sophie, who was standing by the window. Her hair was scooped into a loose knot, revealing the fine bone structure of her face. She looked fragile and vulnerable, and as he watched her he felt a curious ache in his chest.

'When I said last night that we needed to talk, I had no idea how urgent our conversation would be—or its subject,' he said drily.

It was impossible to guess from his unfathomable expression what he was thinking, but Sophie wondered if he was angry. At least he had not asked if the child was his, she thought heavily. But even if he acknowledged responsibility for her pregnancy it did not follow that he planned to stick around. He had distanced himself from his father and the other members of his family, and nothing in his hard features indicated that he wanted his baby.

She gave a bitter laugh. 'It's ironic—Richard broke up with me because he wanted children. You, on the other hand, are probably planning how quickly you can get out of my flat and away from me and our unplanned child.'

Nicolo's gut clenched as he heard the pain in her voice. 'I'm not planning on going anywhere,' he assured her.

'You can't tell me you're not furious.'

He shrugged. 'I have no right to be angry. It was me who was careless.'

She looked at him uncertainly, taken aback by his apparent acceptance of the situation. 'How *do* you feel?'

Nicolo guessed his feelings were similar to those of most men when they heard that they were going to be a father. Initial disbelief had given way to dizzying shock and a sense that he was as helpless as a worm on a hook that had been cast into a very deep ocean. But he also felt something that he could not define, a curious sense of inevitability. All his adult life he had rejected responsibility, but he could not, would not, reject his child.

'What's done is done,' he said quietly. 'Now we have to decide what we are going to do.' He gave Sophie an intense look. 'How do you feel about being pregnant?'

His question threw her, and forced Sophie to examine her feelings.

'I don't know. I think I'm still in shock. When Hugh broke the news I was so relieved that I don't have cancer that the implications of being pregnant didn't really hit me,' she admitted. 'It doesn't seem real. The tests I had a couple of years ago indicated that it was almost impossible for me to conceive.'

She sighed. 'I'd hoped to be able to tell Richard that there was a possibility I might be able to have a baby. But the tests showed that I wasn't ovulating. There seemed no hope that I could be a mother, and it was only fair to tell Richard the truth. I hadn't realised until then that having children was so important to him.' She looked down at her tightly linked fingers. 'I couldn't blame him for ending our relationship, but it…it hurt to know that I wasn't good enough for him, that I was…defective.'

Once again the pain in her voice made Nicolo's gut twist. 'The guy was a jerk,' he said curtly.

Sophie swallowed. 'I realise it's a miracle I conceived and I know I should be over the moon but…I'm stunned.

I never expected to have a child, and instead of having a family, I'd planned a different life of travel and adventure.' She grimaced. 'I've booked to go on a hot-air balloon flight over the Serengeti next spring, but I won't be able to go when I'm eight months pregnant.'

Panic swept through Sophie and suddenly she could not hold back her emotions. 'I feel trapped,' she admitted huskily. 'I don't know how to be a mother. When I've visited my friends who have children I've wondered how they cope with a baby that cries all the time.'

For Sophie, who prided herself on her efficiency and capability to deal with any work situation, the feeling that she would not be able to cope with the demands of motherhood was truly terrifying. For the first time since she was sixteen she burst into tears. 'If you want the truth, Nicolo,' she choked, 'I'm scared.'

As he watched Sophie's face crumple Nicolo felt a dull ache in his heart. He had done this to her. He had caused this strong, beautiful woman to cry. He strode across the room and drew her into his arms.

'I don't know what to do,' she sobbed.

For a split second, coldness invaded Nicolo's heart as it occurred to him that perhaps she was considering not allowing the pregnancy to continue. Even more shocking was how much he cared. He had never thought about having a child, but the knowledge that his baby was developing inside her evoked a primitive protective instinct in him.

'I'll have to look for another job. Christos travels so much and I'll need to settle in one place. And I'll need to find somewhere else to live so that the baby can have its own room.'

'Shh,' he soothed, stroking her silky honey-gold hair as the tension left him. He was ashamed he had doubted her. After all she had been through, Sophie was understandably shocked to be pregnant, but he did not doubt that she would be a devoted mother. He thought of his own mother, who had left her children, who had abandoned him when he had needed her so desperately after the fire. Many years had passed since his mother had gone, but it still hurt and he would always miss her.

He looked down at Sophie. She would never abandon her child. He knew it with a certainty that shook him. Seeing her crying evoked a fiercely protective instinct in him. Did she really think he would leave her to bring up their child alone?

It was understandable that she doubted his commitment when she considered his track record, he acknowledged grimly. It occurred to Nicolo then that he needed to think very hard about what he could offer Sophie. His financial support was unquestionable, but their child needed more important things than money. Some of his old feelings of self-doubt returned. But he realised that for his child's sake he must deal with the demons of his past once and for all and take control of his future.

'I'm all right now.' Sophie eased out of Nicolo's arms and wiped her tears away with unsteady fingers. It had felt so good to rest her cheek against his chest and listen to the steady thud of his heart. For a few moments she had imagined what it would be like if they were a normal couple who were celebrating the news that they were expecting their first child. How wonderful it would be to feel protected and cherished by the father of her baby. Common sense kicked in and she stepped away from Nicolo, feeling embarrassed by her display of emotions.

She gave him a tremulous smile. 'I guess I'm still in shock. But I'll be fine,' she assured him.

Nicolo believed her. He knew that Sophie's brief flash

of weakness was only temporary and once she had got herself together she would manage perfectly well without him.

'It's only natural that you're feeling emotional,' he murmured. He scooped her into his arms, ignoring her startled gasp, and carried her through to the bedroom where he placed her on the bed and pulled the sheet over her. 'I want you to know that you can rely on me, Sophie,' he told her seriously. 'I'm going to take care of you.'

His beguiling words tugged on Sophie's heart, but she reminded herself that Nicolo's kindness was simply because he felt responsible for her. 'I don't need to be taken care of,' she said stiffly. 'The sickness should pass in the next few weeks and it's perfectly all right for me to go to work as usual.'

Nicolo ignored her protest, and Sophie's eyes widened as she watched him open the wardrobe and take out her suitcase. 'What are you doing?' she demanded as he proceeded to take clothes from the hangers and shove them into the case.

'I'm packing some clothes for you to bring to Chatsfield House. You won't be able to commute from Buckinghamshire to London every day, and the break from work will do you good.' He leaned across the bed and slid his hand beneath her chin, tilting her face so that she was forced to meet his gaze.

'We need to talk, Sophie, and work out how we are going to bring up our child.'

'*We* are going to bring up our child?' she said faintly. It had not occurred to her that he might want to be involved.

'Our baby deserves to be loved and cared for by both of his or her parents, don't you think?' His warm breath whispered across Sophie's lips and she hardly dared to breathe, wishing he would kiss her. She felt a sharp stab of disappointment when he straightened up and walked over to the door. 'I'm going to make you some lunch, and then I'm going to take you home with me.'

He hesitated in the doorway and turned to look at her, his expression guarded, hiding his thoughts. 'Your pregnancy might be unplanned, but I promise I will take care of you and our child, Sophie.'

His words sounded like a solemn vow but they chilled Sophie's heart. The child inside her had been created during a passion-filled night that she and Nicolo had shared. But the next morning he had sent her away because he had not wanted a relationship with her. Now, because of the baby, he felt bound to her by duty, and it was that knowledge that caused tears to slip silently down her cheeks the instant he walked out of the room.

Nicolo drove down the lane leading to Chatsfield House and cursed beneath his breath as the Jeep shook violently when one of the wheels hit a pothole. He vowed to himself that he would hire contractors to repair the road. He glanced at Sophie sitting in the passenger seat. She had slept for most of the journey to Buckinghamshire but now she opened her eyes and looked around as he steered through the tunnel of trees.

She was wearing jeans and a soft pink sweater and did not look at all pregnant, but Nicolo supposed it would be a few months before she showed signs that his child was growing inside her. *His child...* His hands tightened on the steering wheel. It still seemed unreal. Yet when he studied Sophie more closely he noticed that her breasts beneath her clingy sweater looked fuller and her face was softer somehow, as if she was concealing a miraculous secret.

She gave a tiny yawn. 'Who looked after Dorcha while you were in London?'

'Betty stayed at the house with him.' Nicolo smiled ruefully. 'The dog has been pining for you. He often sits outside your bedroom door, howling.'

'I've missed him too.' She had missed the wolfhound almost as much as she had missed Nicolo, Sophie admitted to herself. Dorcha wasn't the only one who had been pining.

The red-brick house looked as austere as she remembered it, but she was glad to be back in Buckinghamshire. Nicolo opened the front door and they were immediately greeted by an ecstatic Dorcha, who barked madly until Sophie made a fuss of him.

'I'll take him to the garden,' she said. 'I could do with stretching my legs after sitting in the car.'

The lawn still looked like a wild meadow, but when she strolled down to the swimming pool she discovered that it was now fully restored and the clear blue water looked inviting.

'The weather is still warm enough to use the pool,' Nicolo said when he joined her. 'We could swim now, if you like?'

'Maybe tomorrow,' Sophie decided quickly. 'I'm tired.' More to the point, she knew she would be unable to keep her eyes, and quite probably her hands, off Nicolo if he was half-naked, wearing only a pair of swim shorts. She bit her lip. 'I still can't believe that this is happening. I keep thinking that I'll wake up and find it was all a dream.'

Nicolo shot a glance at her troubled face and felt a surge of guilt, aware that his irresponsibility was to blame for the situation they were now in. Sophie had believed she was infertile, and he had known that when he had made love to her without protection.

'Do you wish it was a dream?' he asked quietly. 'Don't you want the baby?'

Was it selfish to admit that she wished she could have her old life back—a fulfilling career, travel to far-flung corners of the globe, adventurous friends who were not tied down with the responsibility of a child? Sophie knew that her pregnancy was a million to one chance, a miracle. But a little part of her could not help thinking that it was a disaster.

'I don't know,' she told Nicolo with painful honesty.

They walked back to the house in silence, and Sophie wished she knew what he was thinking. 'What shall I cook for dinner?'

'It'll have to be steak, I'm afraid. That's all that's in the fridge.'

'Oh, well, the iron will probably be good for the baby anyway,' she said wryly.

Nicolo shook his head. 'I can see I'm going to need to make some changes at Chatsfield House, starting with employing a few more staff, including a housekeeper and cook. You might not feel like cooking when you're busy with a new baby,' he told Sophie.

Her steps faltered. 'I don't know where I'll live with the baby once it's born, but it's unlikely to be in Buckinghamshire. I'll need to be closer to London for work.'

He frowned. 'You won't be able to work for the first few months after the baby arrives. You can hardly take a newborn infant into the office.'

'Obviously I'll have to find a good nursery.' Sophie rubbed her brow. 'I haven't had a chance to think about how I'll manage.' It was all very well for Nicolo to criticise, but the responsibility of caring for their child would fall mainly to her. 'Do you have any suggestions?' she snapped.

'Yes, you can live here with me.'

If only Nicolo had made that suggestion after they had

slept together, she thought sadly. Unfortunately he was five weeks too late. 'It's not what you would have chosen. You like living alone,' she reminded him.

If that was true, then why had he missed Sophie so much since she had left him that he'd felt as if a lead weight had taken up residence in his chest? Nicolo brooded.

'Things are going to be different from now on, and we will both have to make adjustments and compromises,' he said tersely.

Later that evening, as they ate steak with Béarnaise sauce in the dining room, Sophie remembered Nicolo's extreme reaction when she had been about to light a candle. He had been left with physical and emotional scars from the fire years ago, and she was afraid that he would never come to terms with his guilt that he had started the blaze which had had such devastating consequences for him and the chambermaid.

'Why were you so angry with your father when you went to his penthouse suite at the hotel?'

Nicolo had once accused her of asking too many questions, but she sensed that the explanation behind this was crucial for her to be able to understand him better. After all, Nicolo was going to be a father himself in a few months, and understanding his complex character was vital if they were both going to be involved in their child's upbringing.

He was silent for several minutes. 'I've never told anyone—including my father—what I am about to tell you,' he said finally. Nicolo exhaled deeply. 'A week before the fire I had gone to stay at the Chatsfield London. Gene was more or less living there permanently. It was a year after my mother had left the family and disappeared. Lucilla was doing her best to look after the younger ones here because my father was apparently too busy running the hotels to have time for his children.

'I didn't tell him about my visit. I wanted to surprise him.' He grimaced. 'Instead it was me who had the surprise. I had a key to the penthouse and I let myself in. I heard my father's voice from the bedroom—and a woman's voice.' He gave Sophie a resigned look. 'I should have left then, but I was curious. The bedroom door was half-open and when I looked in I saw my father naked in bed with one of the hotel's chambermaids.'

'Oh, no!' Sophie could imagine how shocked and horrified a thirteen-year-old boy must have felt.

'They didn't notice me as I slipped out of the penthouse. No one knew what I had seen. But I realised that the rumours I had heard about my father having affairs with other women—which I hadn't believed—must be true. I was convinced that my mother had discovered my father's infidelity, and that was the reason she had left. She adored my father but he had broken her heart and I did not blame her for wanting to get away from the pain and humiliation he had caused her.

'I hated my father for what he had done,' Nicolo admitted roughly. 'I felt betrayed. I'd hero-worshipped Gene but now I had seen that he was a liar and a cheat and I wanted to hurt him like he had hurt my mother.'

'So you went back to the penthouse to tip his whisky collection away, and you inadvertently started the fire.' Sophie sighed. 'You were a child, Nicolo, a young boy who felt let down by the person you should have been able to trust. But the past is history and your father is an old man. Maybe it's time you forgave him.'

A week ago, even a day ago, Nicolo would have rejected Sophie's suggestion. He had been angry with his father for so many years, but now he was going to be a father himself and he found his attitude towards Gene softening. People made mistakes. Perhaps his father had regrets about the past. Nicolo had refused to listen when Gene had tried to talk to him. *Dio*, for nearly twenty years he had pushed his father away. He hoped that if he made mistakes in the future, his child would be more forgiving of him.

'I want to be a good father,' he told Sophie gruffly. He reached across the table and took her hand in his.

'We have a duty to try to be the best parents we can be. Every decision we make from now on must be in the interest of the child. Do you agree?'

Sophie stared down at their linked fingers. Her heart had leapt when Nicolo had clasped her hand, but now she felt trapped by his firm grip. He was holding her fingers as though he never wanted to let her go—but it wasn't her he wanted. He simply felt duty-bound to take care of her because she was pregnant with his baby. The realisation felt like an arrow through her heart.

'You're right, of course,' she muttered as she got up from the table. 'But the baby isn't due for another eight months and we have plenty of time to decide how we are going to manage things.

'It's been a busy day.' She ignored the thought that she had slept in the car for a chunk of it. For some reason she felt like crying, and whether or not pregnancy hormones were to blame for her ragged emotions she did not want to break down in front of Nicolo. 'I'm going to bed,' she announced abruptly.

Sophie searched around the guest bedroom she had occupied the last time she had stayed at Chatsfield House, wondering where Nicolo had put her suitcase. The bed was unmade and she would have to collect clean sheets from the laundry cupboard—unless he assumed…

Her heart was thudding as she walked along the landing and knocked on the door of his room. The first thing she saw when she walked in was her suitcase lying empty on the floor. Her eyes flew to Nicolo, who was sprawled on the bed.

'What have you done with my clothes?'

'I unpacked for you and put your things in my spare wardrobe.' He gave her a bland smile but the expression in his eyes was watchful and faintly predatory, and Sophie sensed that if she attempted to leave the room he would spring up with the speed of a panther and stop her.

She could feel the pulse at the base of her throat beating erratically. 'You said that spending one night together was fun, but two would be foolish,' she reminded him.

His eyes glinted. 'Perhaps we are both foolish then, Sophie, because last night was our second night together and we proved when we made love at your flat that we can't resist each other.'

Tonight, more than ever, he looked like the highwayman of Sophie's imagination. With his loose white silk shirt unbuttoned to halfway down his chest and his long dark hair falling over his collar he looked indolent and so dangerously sexy that desire tugged swift and sharp in the pit of her stomach. She could feel her resolve to keep her distance from him crumbling.

'What would a third night be?' she could not prevent herself from asking.

His smile softened, and his voice deepened and became lush and beguiling. 'Inevitable,' he murmured.

He stood up and crossed the room in long strides to stand in front of her, but did not touch her. He simply stared down at her as if he was waiting for her to decide what should happen next, as if he was giving her a choice.

'The only reason you brought me to Chatsfield House is because I'm carrying your baby,' she whispered.

'I didn't know you were pregnant when I came to your flat yesterday. I didn't know when I made love to you. All I knew was that I'd missed you like hell,' he said roughly. 'Believe it or not, I had every intention of asking you to come back to me.'

Sophie bit her lip, torn between wanting to believe him, and the voice of caution inside her head which pointed out that when Nicolo said he'd missed her he was talking about their physical attraction. Sex was not a basis for a relationship. She did not even know what sort of relationship she wanted with him. If she hadn't been pregnant, would she have agreed to come back to Chatsfield House?

Of course she would have, she thought with a rueful sigh. She had ached for him for five long weeks, and she ached for him now. She could not deny the truth to herself when her body was responding to his nearness. Her breasts felt heavy and her nipples were already hardening in anticipation of him caressing them with his hands and mouth.

He lifted his hand and cradled her cheek. The gesture was unexpectedly tender and when she looked into his eyes she glimpsed something in his expression that tugged on her heart. She could not help herself, and took a tiny step towards him. It was the sign Nicolo had been hoping for. With a muffled groan he drew her into his arms and slanted his mouth over hers.

The last time she had been in his room he had rejected her. Sophie blocked out the memory as Nicolo kissed her with increasing passion, as if he was deliberately trying to make up for his coldness when he had sent her away. He traced his hands over her body, removing her clothes so that he could reacquaint himself with her slender shape and discover the new fullness of her breasts. Pregnancy had made her nipples ultrasensitive, and she gasped when he gently teased each taut peak with his tongue before he suckled her, creating exquisite sensations that arced down to her pelvis.

When he laid her on the bed Sophie reached for him and pulled him down onto her eager body. It was easier not to think about the future, and instead she became a slave to Nicolo's sensual foreplay as he aroused her with his clever fingers and then lowered his head between her legs and brought her almost to the edge of heaven with his tongue.

As the first ripples of her orgasm ran through her she clutched his shoulders and wrapped her legs around his back as he surged forward. In the moment that their bodies became one she felt a connection with him that went beyond their physical union. He was the father of the baby developing inside her and Sophie realised that they would be forever linked by their child.

CHAPTER ELEVEN

OVER THE FOLLOWING weeks Sophie purposefully did not allow herself to think about the future that seemed frighteningly uncertain. Hugh Bryant arranged for her to have an early ultrasound scan. 'There is no evidence to show that the chemotherapy you received could cause any abnormalities in the baby,' he assured her. 'But obviously it's a good idea to monitor your pregnancy closely.'

Nicolo drove her to a hospital in London for the scan. At this early stage of her pregnancy the baby was no more than a tiny blob shaped like a kidney bean, and the sonographer explained that the regular flutter they could see was the baby's heartbeat. The evidence of the miracle of new life was beautiful and awe-inspiring and Sophie tried to feel excited, but she still felt apprehensive and trapped at the prospect of being a single mother.

Her life would never be the same again and she felt resentful that Nicolo's life would not be as affected as hers would be. They had not discussed the baby since he had insisted that he wanted to be involved in their child's upbringing, but she assumed he intended to offer financial assistance and perhaps arrange visitation rights. No doubt they would be able to come to an amicable arrangement, she thought dully. She told herself she should be glad that he was prepared to stand by her, but deep down she wished that things were different and they were a normal couple who were looking forward to having a baby together.

Back at Chatsfield House she deliberately switched her mind off, and once she'd stopped worrying, she found it surprisingly easy to relax. Maybe it was her body's natural defence mechanism in the early stages of pregnancy, she mused. Christos was still in Greece and Jessie seemed to be handling both Lucilla's and Christos's calls well enough.

Nicolo had hired a friendly new cook, Joan, and her husband, George, who was a gardener. The transformation to the garden was amazing, no longer a wilderness but a beautiful place to sit and admire the roses. The golden days of late summer drifted past. Although Sophie was sometimes sick first thing in the morning the nausea soon passed and with the help of Joan's wonderful dinners the waistband on her jeans started to feel tight.

The reminder that her pregnancy was progressing forced Sophie to face up to reality. She could not continue to live with Nicolo indefinitely. He still spent many hours working in his study, but to her surprise and secret delight he spent a lot of time with her. The weather continued to be warm and they swam in the pool every afternoon. Sometimes they made love on a sun lounger, or lying on the cool green grass, and every night became a feast for Sophie's senses as Nicolo used all his skill to excite and arouse her.

Pregnancy had certainly not affected her libido, she thought ruefully. She lived for those moments of pleasure in Nicolo's arms. The long nights of making love left her body utterly sated but her heart achingly empty. It was her own fault for falling in love with him, she reminded herself. Nicolo had opened up to her, probably more than he had done with anyone else, but he was still a reclusive, enigmatic man who had cut himself off from his emotions and she doubted he would ever change.

Nicolo pushed open the gate to the walled garden and felt a familiar tightening sensation in his stomach when he saw Sophie sitting on a bench beneath the willow tree. He'd guessed he would find her here. She came most mornings to read in the peaceful garden his mother had created many years ago.

She was unaware of his presence and he allowed himself a few moments to study her. *Beautiful* did not begin to describe her. He moved his eyes possessively over her, from her silky honey-gold hair rippling past her shoulders, to the new luscious fullness of her breasts. She was still slim now, but in a few more months her belly would be swollen with his child. The knowledge filled Nicolo with fierce pride and excitement, but he sensed that Sophie did not share his feelings. At the scan appointment she had looked tense, and since then, whenever he mentioned the baby she quickly changed the subject.

She looked up as he walked along the gravel path towards her, and he noticed that her laptop computer was open.

He frowned. 'I thought one of the junior secretaries was dealing with any work that Giatrakos sends through from Greece?'

'Jessie is covering for me, but she can't continue to act as Christos's PA indefinitely—after all, she works for Lucilla. There's no reason why I can't return to work, especially now that I'm no longer suffering from morning sickness. I've been lucky. Some women experience nausea for months during their pregnancy.'

Sophie saw Nicolo glance at her laptop screen. 'I'm

looking on estate agents' websites,' she explained. 'I'll need to live close to London for my job, but rents are cheaper in the suburbs and I should be able to find a two-bedroom flat for roughly the same rent as I'm paying now.'

Despite the heat of the sultry summer's day, coldness invaded Nicolo's heart. 'If you move out of London you'll have a longer commute,' he said curtly.

'That's true.' And public transport would be another expense to cover. Sophie's brow pleated. 'But I don't see what else I can do.'

Nicolo stared at the intricate design of box hedges that formed the knot garden. He remembered his mother had planted every shrub herself. She had poured her love into this garden and it seemed a fitting place for him to put his past behind him and look to the future.

'You don't have to work. There is an obvious solution that will enable us to both be part of our child's life.' He sensed the question hovering on Sophie's lips and took a swift breath. 'I think we should get married.'

The silence seemed to bounce off the walls of the enclosed garden. Sophie ignored the painful lurch her heart gave and stared at Nicolo. He had not actually proposed to her, she reminded herself. He had simply suggested marriage out of a misguided belief that it would be in the best interest of their child.

'A shotgun wedding is not an obvious solution as far as I'm concerned,' she said tautly. 'It's a crazy idea.'

'It wouldn't be a shotgun wedding. And why is the idea of us marrying crazy?'

'*Why?* Well—because…' She shook her head. 'Nicolo, when your parents got married I assume they were in love. They certainly looked happy in their wedding photo. But even though they loved each other, their marriage didn't last. Neither did my parents' relationship, despite the fact that they were madly in love when they married.'

Nicolo was curious when he heard a tremor in her voice. 'Why did your parents break up?'

'For the same reason your parents did, I guess. My father had an affair.' Sophie bit her lip as raw memories resurfaced. 'It happened while I was ill. Mum spent a lot of time at the hospital with me while I was having chemo. My dad visited me, of course, but he had to carry on working full-time.'

She sighed. 'It must have been a very stressful time for both of them. Dad disliked going home to an empty house after work, and so he started taking his new secretary out to dinner. He said they were just friends to start with. But then he fell in love.'

She turned towards Nicolo, her eyes blazing. 'My father admitted that my illness had made him think about his own mortality. He realised that he hadn't been happy with my mother, and he decided to seize his chance of happiness with his lover.' She gave a mirthless laugh. 'You can't imagine how I felt, knowing that my parents' divorce and my mum's unhappiness were my fault. If I hadn't developed cancer, maybe Dad would have stayed with us. You're not the only one to have a guilt complex,' she said bleakly.

'That's ridiculous—you couldn't help getting cancer.' Nicolo heard the devastation in Sophie's voice and he felt a strange sensation in his chest, as if his heart was being squeezed in a vice. 'Perhaps your illness was a catalyst, but if your father was unhappy being married to your mother he would have left at some point.'

Sophie sighed. 'What I'm trying to say is that it would be a bad idea for us to get married because I'm pregnant when we don't—' she hesitated, suddenly afraid that she might give herself away '—have feelings for each other.' She faltered. 'If marriages between people who started out in love don't last, what hope would there be for us? I believe it will be better for us to remain as friends rather than risk putting our child through the misery of us divorcing sometime in the future.'

Nicolo frowned. 'That's a very negative attitude.' In truth he was taken aback by her refusal. But when had Sophie ever acted as he expected her to do, as most other women would do? he thought wryly. He had been so focused on what a huge deal it was for him to offer to make a commitment to Sophie and his child that he hadn't considered she might turn him down. She was not good for his ego, he thought self-derisively.

'I'm being realistic.' Resigned to the truth was perhaps a better explanation, Sophie thought dully. She did not want to marry a man who did not love her. So why was her heart longing to agree to Nicolo's suggestion and hope that in time he would come to care for her?

'I'm not convinced that marriage is really what you want,' she said huskily. 'You're still haunted by your past. You shut yourself away from the outside world. More importantly, you shut yourself off from people who care about you—your family. Your inability to forgive yourself for events that happened years ago will eventually make you cold and bitter. How can I believe that you will love our child when I've seen no evidence that you are capable of love?'

'*Dio*, Sophie!' Nicolo jerked to his feet. 'That's unfair. Of course I will love our child.' He stared in frustration at her disbelieving expression. 'I am not the person I once was. I admit I was so bound up in my guilt that I could not look to the future. But I've changed. *You* changed me.' His voice deepened. 'You helped me to see myself differently.'

He hesitated. 'It's not true to say that I shut myself off from the outside world.'

He wanted to tell Sophie about the financial support he had given to the Michael Morris Burns Support Foundation for the past eight years, and his recent decision to become the public figurehead of the charity. But a glance at his watch told him that he did not have time to talk to her properly now. It was important that he arrive in London in time for the press conference to explain about the work and aims of the burns charity.

The conversation with Sophie would have to wait until he came back tomorrow. Perhaps then he would be able to show her that he had changed from the surly man who had thrown her out of Chatsfield House when she had first arrived. He might even be able to convince her that he would be a devoted father and a good husband—something he had clearly failed to do so far, Nicolo thought heavily.

'Do you remember I mentioned that I might have to go to London for a meeting?' he murmured. 'The meeting is today. I've arranged to stay in town tonight and I'll come back in the morning. We'll talk more then.' He looked at Sophie's tense face and felt a strong urge to cancel his plans and stay with her. But everything was set up for the press conference and he hoped the publicity would generate vital support for the charity.

'Will you be all right? George and Joan have gone to visit their daughter for a couple of days and you'll be here on your own.'

Sophie gave a listless shrug as she watched Nicolo check the time again. He was obviously impatient to get away from her. He had not tried to persuade her to marry him and he was probably relieved that she had turned him down.

'I'll have Dorcha with me.' She glanced at the wolf-hound sprawled on the grass at her feet. 'He would terrify any intruders.'

'He didn't scare you,' Nicolo said drily. He leaned down and brushed his mouth over hers in a kiss that held both passion and a tenderness that made Sophie's heart ache. She could not define the expression in his eyes when he said softly, 'I quickly discovered that you are unique, Sophie. I've never met anyone like you before.'

Hours later, Sophie still could not decide whether Nicolo's parting remark had been a compliment or criticism. What did it matter? she thought wearily. He did not love her and that was all that mattered. It was the reason she had refused to marry him.

It was hot and humid in the garden and not much cooler inside the house. The weather forecast predicted storms, and from the look of the ominous purple clouds gathering on the hills like a mustering army, it seemed that the late-summer heatwave was about to break.

Sophie felt too churned up to want to eat, but she reminded herself that she had a duty to feed the baby growing inside her and made herself a cheese salad. *Duty* was such a passionless word, she mused. Nicolo clearly believed it was his duty to offer to marry her. She wondered if he would still be prepared to support her and their child, or whether the fact that she had turned him down meant he no longer felt it was necessary to stand by her.

No, he would not abandon her, she thought with fierce certainty. Nicolo was an honourable man, and having been abandoned by his mother when he had been a boy

Sophie was convinced he would not walk away from his own child. When he returned tomorrow they would have to start making plans about where their child would live, and where he or she would spend birthdays and Christmases. Her heart sank as she recalled the last, uncomfortable Christmas she had spent with her father and his new family.

Her hand crept to her stomach, and for the first time since she had discovered she was pregnant she imagined the baby as a little person. Was passing the child between her and Nicolo like a parcel the best they could do? But was the alternative of a loveless marriage any better? she wondered dully.

Desperate to find something to occupy her thoughts, she switched on the TV to catch the evening news programme.

Nicolo was overwhelmed by memories as he walked across the foyer of the Chatsfield Hotel. He had not been back here since the fire nineteen years ago, but the hotel felt as familiar as he remembered from his childhood. It was true the decor had been updated but the ambiance of luxury and exclusivity created by the Italian marble floors and ornate crystal chandeliers hanging from the ceiling was pure Chatsfield style.

When he stepped into the lift, the Chatsfield signature scent diffused through the air conditioning sent his mind hurtling back in time. As the lift rose towards the top floor and the penthouse suite Nicolo felt his tension increase. The last time he had made this journey he had been a teenage boy intent on mischief. He could not have known that on that fateful night his life and the life of a young chambermaid would change for ever.

His thoughts turned to the visit he had paid Marissa Bisek after the press conference. He had not dared try to imagine how she would react to his confession that he had been responsible for the fire in which they had both nearly died but his conscience had decided that he must tell Marissa the truth.

She had been pleased to see him, and welcomed him into her home. Looking at her scarred face, Nicolo had told himself he could not blame her if she hated him once she had learned the truth, but to his shock Marissa had hugged him and insisted that she had nothing to forgive him for. He had saved her life, and she would always be grateful to him. If it had not been for his bravery, she'd said, she would not have seen her youngest son, who had been a baby at the time of the fire, graduate from university. Marissa also revealed that she was about to get married to a wonderful man who loved her and did not care about her scars.

'I am so happy with my life,' she told Nicolo. 'I hope you can put the past behind you and find happiness and love.'

Her words had lifted a great weight from Nicolo's shoulders. Like Sophie, Marissa appreciated how precious life was and had chosen to live every day to the full. Nicolo felt humbled by the strength of both women. He had searched his soul and acknowledged that Sophie had been right when she'd said that he must stop punishing himself for what he had done in the past and should embrace the future.

Her advice was even more important now that his future included being a father to their child. But before he could move forward he knew he had to confront his father about Gene's infidelity that Nicolo was certain had been the reason his mother had abandoned the Chatsfield family.

It took all his nerve to enter the penthouse which had

been the scene of such terror and pain when he had been a boy. His father stood up from the sofa and greeted him with a hesitant smile. Gene had sounded surprised when he had phoned earlier to ask if he could visit. As Nicolo walked towards his father he was struck by the fact that Gene was an elderly man. He was still a charismatic figure and his eyes were a bright, piercing blue, but his hair was silver and he stooped slightly as he stepped forward.

'Nicolo.' Gene held his arms out. 'I saw your press conference. I had no idea that you had set up a charity to help burns victims. Why have you kept your work as a fundraiser secret until now?' He placed his hands on Nicolo's shoulders. 'I am so proud of you, as are the rest of the family.' His voice became husky. 'Your mother would have been proud too, my son.'

Santa Madre! Nicolo felt choked with emotion. He had come here to demand answers from his father. He had planned to reveal how he had seen Gene in bed with a young maid in the penthouse all those years ago, and how angry and betrayed he had felt by his father's behaviour. But Sophie's words flashed into his mind.

The past is history. Maybe it's time you forgave your father.

Maybe his forgiveness was long overdue, Nicolo acknowledged. He did not know what happened between his parents. As a boy he had blamed his father for driving his mother away, but as an adult he understood that relationships were complex and love was fragile and needed to be nurtured by both partners.

Swallowing hard, Nicolo stepped into his father's embrace and hugged the elderly man. 'Papa,' he said softly, 'I have something to tell you. In a few months' time you are going to be a grandfather.'

* * *

At Chatsfield House Sophie watched the news programme with a heavy heart. She was about to change channels when a familiar face flashed onto the screen.

She tensed with shock. *What on earth was Nicolo doing on TV?*

He seemed to be giving a press conference, and he looked gorgeous, Sophie thought numbly as she stared at his image. Wearing a charcoal-grey suit and light blue shirt, it was easy to believe he was a billionaire financier, but his rugged features and overlong hair still reminded her of a highwayman.

Nicolo looked into the camera as he spoke.

'I established the Michael Morris Burns Support Foundation with the help of Michael's sister, Beth Doyle. For the past eight years, Beth has filled the role of chief executive of the foundation, and she has worked incredibly hard to heighten public awareness of the vital help that the charity gives to burns victims. However, Beth has decided to step down as head of the foundation so that she can concentrate on her family,' Nicolo explained. 'I will now combine my role as fundraising director with the duties of CEO, and oversee the running of every aspect of the charity. I will continue to work tirelessly for the foundation, and I look forward to my role as public figurehead of the charity.'

Sophie continued to stare at the screen long after Nicolo's image had been replaced by a chirpy woman giving the weather forecast. He was the new public figurehead of a charity! Guilt swept through her when she remembered how she had accused him of shutting himself away from the outside world. Nothing could be further from the truth. She had also accused him of being haunted by his past, but it was clear that he was determined to use his experience to help other burns victims. Even his career as a financial trader was not to earn money for himself but for the charity where he had been a fundraising director for the past eight years.

Why hadn't he told her about his charity work? Sophie grimaced. Obviously he had not felt comfortable to talk to her about his role within the burns foundation. He was an intensely private man, but it hurt that he had excluded her from something that was so important to him.

She felt ashamed that she had judged him so harshly. He had told her he had changed, but she hadn't believed him, and she hadn't given him a chance. And why was that? Sophie remorselessly questioned herself. The answer shamed her even more. She had wanted him to say that he loved her, and when he hadn't she had been coldly dismissive because she had wanted to hurt him for unwittingly breaking her heart.

Right at that moment Sophie did not like herself very much. She went to bed with a heavy heart, hoping for the oblivion of sleep, but after an hour of tossing and turning she selected some music, put her earphones in and lay back down, sternly telling herself that crying all night would not do her or the baby any good.

The storm broke as Nicolo drove along the motorway on his way back to Buckinghamshire late at night. In the distance he saw several jagged flashes of lightning, and the growl of thunder even drowned out the engine noise made by his battered old Jeep. When the baby was born he would have to buy a newer car, he decided.

It was not raining yet, and because the Jeep did not have air conditioning, the sultry air was stifling. Nicolo pressed his foot down on the accelerator as he thought of Sophie alone at Chatsfield House. Not that she would be afraid of a storm, he acknowledged. Sophie was as brave as a lioness—and unfortunately as stubborn as a mule. He should have known that persuading her to marry him would not be an easy task, but he had hoped she would agree for the baby's sake.

He had used her pregnancy as an excuse, he acknowledged. 'Have you actually told Sophie how you feel?' Beth had asked him when he had phoned her after the press conference.

'Not in so many words,' he had admitted. He did not feel comfortable talking about his feelings.

'Perhaps you should try,' Beth had advised gently. 'You don't have to use many words. Three little ones will probably be sufficient.'

Nicolo knew he must overcome the demons that still tormented him and his fear of being rejected, because of his mother. A nerve flickered in his cheek as he thought of the women he had met in his wild years who had been repulsed by his scars. He had laughed off the looks of horror in their eyes, and their pity. But deep down, he had been wounded.

The Beast had retreated to his lair, until one day Beauty had trespassed on his home, and very soon on his heart. But that was where reality differed from the fairy tale. He and Sophie were not going to live happily ever after. She did not want to marry him and insisted that she was perfectly capable of bringing up their child on her own.

His jaw clenched. There had been a few occasions during the time they had been living together when he had caught her looking at him with an expression in her eyes that had made him wonder....

The only thing he could do was be honest about his feelings. But laying himself open to rejection was not easy for a man who had suppressed his emotions for almost two decades.

Nicolo turned off the motorway and a few minutes later he drove through the village. At one o'clock in the morning, the only sign of life was a fox slinking along the grass verge. At the top of the hill he looked down over the dark valley and was puzzled by the curious glow he could see in the distance.

The orange glow became brighter as he wound along the country roads, and when he reached the lane leading to Chatsfield House the brilliant light visible above the treetops filled him with foreboding. Racing on, he rounded the bend and braked hard.

'Santa Madre di Dio!' he whispered fearfully.

CHAPTER TWELVE

CHATSFIELD HOUSE WAS ABLAZE. Stunned by the sight in front of him, Nicolo spoke in his mother's language. He quickly realised the most likely explanation for the fire was that the west tower had been struck by lightning. Much of the brickwork had collapsed and a fire now raged across the roof of the house.

His brain functioned automatically as he pulled out his phone and called the emergency services, giving the necessary details swiftly and efficiently.

Is there anyone in the building? he was asked. When he confirmed that there was one person inside he was advised not to attempt to enter the burning house but to wait for the fire crew.

'Like hell,' Nicolo muttered as he leapt out of the Jeep and ran towards the front door. He could hear Dorcha barking frantically from inside the house. Even if Sophie had slept through the storm, it seemed impossible that she could not hear the racket the wolfhound was making.

Unless she had been overcome by smoke? His blood ran cold, especially when he opened door and was greeted by a thick black cloud.

'Sophie!'

Through the smoke he could see that the ground-floor

rooms were not yet alight, but upstairs the flames were roaring, destroying everything in their path.

'Angel…' For a moment Nicolo was overwhelmed by a feeling of utter despair. Sophie and his unborn child were trapped in the inferno. It was worse than any nightmare. This surely was hell on earth. And perhaps it would be his grave, he thought grimly. If he was unable to rescue Sophie he would die trying.

Holding his jacket over his face, he crossed the hall and stared up at the flames that were already curling around the wooden banister at the top of the staircase. He did not have much time. The heat as he ran up the stairs was unbelievable. He remembered the terror he had felt as a teenager caught in the fire in the penthouse, and he felt the same paralysing fear now as he remembered the pain of his skin blistering, the smell of his burning flesh.

His steps did not falter. Adrenalin pumped through his veins as he reached the landing and saw the true horror of the fire. At the far end of the corridor the ceiling had collapsed and burning roof struts were raining down. Guided by the sound of Dorcha's barks, Nicolo tore down the hallway, ignoring the danger of the flaming debris falling around him. Sophie must have barricaded herself in the bedroom. She must be terrified. Driven by a primal instinct to protect her and his child that she carried, Nicolo forgot his own fear and rushed towards the flames.

Sophie could not understand what was happening. She had been asleep and did not know what had woken her. The room seemed to be filled with a dense haze that was making her eyes sting, and bizarrely, she could hear music.

She suddenly realised she was wearing earphones attached to her music player. The minute she pulled them out she heard Dorcha barking outside the bedroom door. There was another sound too, a strange roaring noise. What on earth? She smelled smoke and began to cough. Heart thumping with panic, she groped her way over to the door and opened it.

The wolfhound threw himself at her. Sophie rubbed his shaggy head, but her eyes were locked on the horrifying sight before her.

'Dear God!' she whispered when she saw flames leaping up the walls, devouring an oil painting and flicking along the ceiling. A wall of fire barred her route to the stairs. Sick fear churned in her stomach when she realised there was no other way down.

'Oh, Dorcha, you were trying to warn me, weren't you?' As she hugged the dog she thought of how devastated Nicolo would be to lose his faithful companion. 'Now we're both trapped,' she choked. Pulling the dog into the room, she shut the door and instinctively hurried over to open the window. Far below was the gravel driveway but there was nothing to cushion her if she jumped. Even if by some miracle she survived, what would happen to the baby?

In that instant Sophie was overwhelmed by a desperate urgency to protect her baby, her little miracle. How could she ever have thought that her pregnancy was an inconvenience? Against huge odds she had been given the chance to be a mother. But now it seemed that neither she nor her child had a chance.

She would never see Nicolo again, never be able to tell him what she should have told him weeks ago. Tears filled her eyes. Her stupid pride had stopped her from telling him that she loved him, and now it was too late....

'Sophie.'

For a moment she thought she had imagined Nicolo's

voice, but as she swung round and peered through the smoke that was rapidly thickening in the bedroom, she saw him standing in the doorway, silhouetted against the flames in the hallway.

'Thank God you're all right.'

'Nicolo…' She could not believe he was real. 'You're in London,' she said inanely.

'I decided to drive back tonight, thankfully.' He strode across the room and stared down at her, a nerve jerking in his cheek. '*Dio*, Sophie—' his voice cracked '—I thought I'd lost you and the baby.'

Of course he was concerned for the baby, Sophie reminded herself. But it did not matter as he snatched her into his arms and held her so tight against his chest that she could feel the powerful beat of his heart.

'By the time I arrived, the fire had already taken hold,' he explained quickly. 'Why didn't you get out of the house while you could?'

'I fell asleep with my earphones in, and I didn't hear Dorcha barking. Nicolo, why did you enter the house if the fire was already serious? It was madness—' her voice caught on a sob '—probably suicide… We can't get out.'

'Do you think I would leave you in danger?' He shook his head, 'No way, angel. I'm going to get you out of here.'

The fire on the roof must have reached the far end of the house and was now above the master bedroom. Sophie screamed as a burning rafter smashed through the ceiling. Shaking with fear, she burrowed closer to Nicolo. 'You shouldn't have risked your life for me.'

He caught hold of her chin and tipped her face up. The room was too dark and full of smoke for her to be able to see his expression, but she heard raw emotion in his voice as he said roughly, 'My life would have no meaning without you.'

'I'm sorry I said those awful things to you,' she whispered brokenly. 'I saw the press conference you gave about the charity you set up to help burns victims. I'm sorry I doubted you.'

'It doesn't matter.' Through the open window Nicolo saw the flashing lights of a fire engine. Relief flooded through him as he leaned out and shouted down to the fire crew.

He tightened his arms around Sophie. 'Do you trust me, angel?'

She felt safe in his arms and knew he would give his life to protect her. 'Of course I trust you.'

Nicolo felt her stiffen as she turned her head and saw the extendable ladder from the fire engine rising towards the window.

Panic gripped Sophie as she watched the ladder coming closer. The fireman standing at the top seemed to be precariously balanced, and the realisation that she would have to join him on the small platform filled her with terror. 'Nicolo…I'm scared.'

'I know, sweetheart, but it's going to be fine. You are going to be rescued first.'

Sophie clutched him. 'Why can't we be rescued together?'

'There's not enough room on the platform. They'll send the ladder back up for me.'

She shook her head. 'I don't want to leave you.'

'You said you trust me.' Nicolo dropped a brief, hard kiss on her mouth before he lifted her up and carried her to the window. 'I promise I'll make it out, Sophie. But I want to know you're safe first.'

What followed became a blur of images as Sophie

stood on the platform with the fireman while the ladder slowly descended. She stared up at the blazing house, her eyes locked on Nicolo. She could see an orange glow behind him and knew the fire must be taking hold in the bedroom. 'Please hurry,' she muttered, urging the ladder to descend quicker so that it could return for Nicolo and Dorcha.

A sudden loud noise shattered the night and she watched in horror as the roof above the bedroom collapsed. Flames leapt towards the sky and black, choking smoke billowed through the open window.

'*Nicolo...Nicolo...*' Sophie screamed his name over and over as her eyes searched desperately for him. But he had disappeared.

Sophie had a vague recollection of travelling in the back of an ambulance, blue flashing lights, being jolted on a trolley as it was pushed through the doors of the accident and emergency unit at the local hospital.

After being checked over by a doctor she was eventually taken to a small private room where the glare of the bright ceiling lights made her eyes water.

'Your eyes are suffering from the effects of the smoke from the fire,' the nurse told her.

Sophie knew that the tears running down her face were for another reason. She sat up on the trolley and clutched the nurse's arm. 'Please, have you heard any news about Mr Chatsfield, the other person who was trapped in the fire?'

'I haven't heard anything yet. But I do have some good news for you,' the nurse told her. 'The ultrasound scan showed that your baby is fine, and doesn't seem to have been affected at all by your awful experience.'

Sophie felt a momentary sense of relief that her little

miracle was still defying the odds. But her joy at hearing the baby was unharmed was replaced with cold dread that there was still no news about Nicolo.

'Miss Ashdown, what are you doing?' the nurse demanded as Sophie slid off the trolley. 'The doctor hasn't discharged you yet.'

'I can't stay here. Where are my shoes?'

'Miss Ashdown, I must insist…'

'You don't understand,' Sophie said fiercely. 'I have to find out what has happened to Nicolo. I need to know if he is alive. And if he's not…' She broke off and closed her eyes as she thought of the terrible, unthinkable possibility that Nicolo had not escaped from the fire.

'*I have to find the man I love,*' she told the nurse. '*Without him, my life might as well be over!*'

'Sophie?'

She jerked her head round and released her breath on a shuddering sigh when she saw Nicolo standing in the doorway. His shirt was ripped and blackened with soot and he had a cut running down one cheek, but he still looked like a devilishly sexy highwayman. Sophie's legs trembled beneath her. 'Thank God,' she said thickly.

'I'll leave the two of you alone,' the nurse murmured, slipping out of the door.

Silence stretched between them, and the noises of the busy casualty unit faded to the background. Sophie swallowed. 'How long have you been standing there?'

'Long enough to hear what you said.' Nicolo's eyes narrowed on her white face. He wondered if she could tell that his heart was slamming violently against his ribcage. 'Did you mean it?'

She stared at his chiselled features and the stern line of his unsmiling mouth, and her stomach plummeted. He had risked his life for her, she reminded herself. He had faced his greatest fear and rushed into a blazing building to save her knowing that he could be burned, and suffer the same agony he had experienced when he had been burned as a teenager.

She lifted her chin and met his gaze, her eyes blazing with emotion.

'Yes, I meant it. I love you with all my heart.' She put her hand up to stop him as he opened his mouth to speak. 'I know you asked me to marry you for the baby's sake—' her voice shook a little '—and I know that you probably don't share my feelings—'

'You don't know anything,' Nicolo interrupted her roughly. 'For a clever woman, you're incredibly slow at working things out.' He closed the gap between them and looked into her eyes and his expression made Sophie's heart tremble.

'You broke into my house and stole my heart,' he told her, his voice as unsteady as Sophie's had been a few moments earlier. 'Right back then, that first day, I knew I was in trouble. That's why I was so determined to make you leave Chatsfield House.'

He threaded his fingers through her honey-gold hair and drew her against him. 'But you refused to go. You thwarted me and irritated me.' He smiled as her eyes flashed at him.

'You made me love you,' he said softly.

Sophie bit her lip. 'If that's true, why did you send me away?'

'I genuinely believed it was best for you.' Nicolo exhaled heavily. 'I doubted myself. I was everything you had accused me of being—remote, aloof, detached from my emotions. But I discovered after you had gone that I wasn't at all detached and I had more emotions than I could handle. I missed you,' he confessed. 'I actually looked forward to the shareholders' meeting because I knew I would see you again. But the meeting was cancelled, so I came to your flat.'

'And discovered that you are going to be a father,' Sophie said drily. 'For someone who has shunned emotional commitment for most of his life, I can understand it was a shock.'

'A wonderful shock,' Nicolo insisted. 'I had never expected to have a child, and I'd never expected to fall in love. I do love you, Sophie,' he whispered against her lips, 'more than you can ever know. I think it's fantastic that we are going to have a baby, but that's not the reason I want to marry you. The truth is that I can't bear the idea of living without you.'

He cradled her face in his hands and gave her a crooked smile that tugged on her heart.

'Will you be my wife, Sophie, and let me love you for the rest of my life?'

'Yes,' she said shakily. 'As long as you understand that I will never stop loving you.'

Tears that she had been struggling to hold back filled her eyes and slid down her cheeks. The memory of seeing the blazing roof of the house collapse—she'd believed onto Nicolo—would be with her for a long time. 'I thought I'd lost you,' she choked.

Nicolo shuddered as he relived the moment when he had discovered the fire and realised that Sophie was trapped inside the house. 'The idea that I might never hold you in my arms again was beyond unbearable.' He brushed her tears away with his thumb pads. 'Don't cry, angel. Or you'll make me cry too.'

Sophie drew a ragged breath when she saw that his lashes were wet, and she hugged him fiercely as if she could somehow imprint her body onto his. 'Once again, by a miracle, our lives have been spared.' She tensed. 'What happened to Dorcha?'

'He's fine, apart from a bit of a singed coat, but luckily his hair is so thick it protected him. He's staying with the vet and I'll pick him up in the morning. Of course we won't be able to return to Chatsfield House until it has been repaired, but I have an idea that I want to discuss with you.'

He looked intently at Sophie, but to her surprise he did not talk about their living arrangements. 'I visited my father yesterday and made my peace with him.'

Her eyes widened. 'Did you tell him that you had seen him with another woman at the penthouse all those years ago?'

'No.' He smiled softly. 'I took your advice and decided to let go of the past. Gene has fallen in love with a charming woman, and they are going to get married. I hope he has many years of happiness ahead of him,' Nicolo said deeply. 'My father is excited at the prospect of being a grandfather. He has suggested donating Chatsfield House to the charity and turning it into a convalescent home specifically for children with burns injuries.'

He dropped a soft kiss on Sophie's mouth. 'I'd like us to buy another house and start off our married life in a home that we've chosen together.'

'I'd like that too.' A thought struck her. 'How will you carry on with your financial trading business if your computers were destroyed?'

'Actually, the fire crew reported that the ground-floor rooms aren't too badly damaged. Anyway, I can run my hedge fund company from any computer. But in future I will spend less time playing the stock markets so that I can concentrate on my role as head of the burns foundation.'

He brushed Sophie's hair back from her face. 'I know

you are going to be busy looking after the baby a few months from now, but if you decide you would like to work too, then there is a vacancy for a PA to the new CEO of the Michael Morris Burns Support Foundation.'

'It sounds interesting.' Sophie stood on tiptoe and linked her arms around Nicolo's neck. 'What would my duties be?' she murmured against his lips.

'To love me with all your heart for eternity, like I promise I will love you.'

She smiled. 'In that case I'm definitely perfect for the position. When can I start?'

'Immediately,' Nicolo said huskily as he claimed her lips in an achingly tender kiss that captured Sophie's heart for ever.

* * * * *

If you enjoyed this book, look out for the next installment of THE CHATSFIELD:
TYCOON'S TEMPTATION *by Trish Morey, coming next month.*

Available August 19, 2014

#3265 TYCOON'S TEMPTATION
The Chatsfield
by Trish Morey

Franco Chatsfield must secure a partnership with Holly Purman's vineyard, the family business she's devoted her whole life to. She'll give Franco six weeks to prove himself, but working together sends their senses reeling—one taste just isn't enough!

#3266 THE HOUSEKEEPER'S AWAKENING
At His Service
by Sharon Kendrick

Injured playboy Luis Martinez is sick of nurses and demands his sweet, innocent housekeeper Carly Conner massage him back to health! Whisked away to the south of France, how long will she be able to deny tantalizing tension between them?

#3267 MORE PRECIOUS THAN A CROWN
by Carol Marinelli

Prince Zahid, heir to the Kingdom of Ishla, once walked away from the fire blazing in Trinity Foster's eyes. Now, after one earth-shattering night, it's revealed that Trinity needs Zahid's protection. She's strictly forbidden, but walking away again may prove impossible....

#3268 CAPTURED BY THE SHEIKH
Rivals to the Crown of Kadar
by Kate Hewitt

Sheikh Khalil's first step to reclaiming his crown is to kidnap his rival's bride-to-be, Elena Karras. Expecting a cold, convenient marriage, this virgin queen is instead carried into the sands, where she discovers an unexpected desire for her sinfully sexy captor!

#3269 A NIGHT IN THE PRINCE'S BED
by Chantelle Shaw

For deaf theater actress Mina Hart, one night with a gorgeous stranger turns into headline news when he's revealed as Prince Aksel of Storvhal. Trapped in icy Scandinavia, can Mina rely on her senses to read this intensely private prince?

#3270 DAMASO CLAIMS HIS HEIR
One Night With Consequences
by Annie West

The virtue behind Princess Marisa's scandalous reputation touched a place in Damaso Pires that he'd thought long destroyed. But their brief affair becomes permanent when Marisa reveals she's pregnant.... There's only one way for Damaso to claim his heir—marriage!

#3271 CHANGING CONSTANTINOU'S GAME
by Jennifer Hayward

All bets are off when reporter Isabel Peters is dropped into Alexios Constantinou's lap during a hellish elevator ride—especially when he discovers that her next story is *him!* With everything at stake, he'll need a whole new game plan....

#3272 THE ULTIMATE REVENGE
The 21st Century Gentleman's Club
by Victoria Parker

Nicandro Santos is determined to bring down the ultra-prestigious *Q Virtus* gentleman's club. But with his enemy's daughter, Olympia Merisi, now in charge, the battle lines between this pair soon blur, and they risk entering more *sensual* territory....

REQUEST YOUR FREE BOOKS!

2 FREE NOVELS PLUS
2 FREE GIFTS!

YES! Please send me 2 FREE Harlequin Presents® novels and my 2 FREE gifts (gifts are worth about $10). After receiving them, if I don't wish to receive any more books, I can return the shipping statement marked "cancel." If I don't cancel, I will receive 6 brand-new novels every month and be billed just $4.30 per book in the U.S. or $4.99 per book in Canada. That's a saving of at least 14% off the cover price! It's quite a bargain! Shipping and handling is just 50¢ per book in the U.S. and 75¢ per book in Canada.* I understand that accepting the 2 free books and gifts places me under no obligation to buy anything. I can always return a shipment and cancel at any time. Even if I never buy another book, the two free books and gifts are mine to keep forever.

106/306 HDN FVRK

Name	(PLEASE PRINT)	
Address		Apt. #
City	State/Prov.	Zip/Postal Code

Signature (if under 18, a parent or guardian must sign)

Mail to the **Harlequin® Reader Service:**
IN U.S.A.: P.O. Box 1867, Buffalo, NY 14240-1867
IN CANADA: P.O. Box 609, Fort Erie, Ontario L2A 5X3

**Are you a current subscriber to Harlequin Presents books
and want to receive the larger-print edition?
Call 1-800-873-8635 or visit www.ReaderService.com.**

* Terms and prices subject to change without notice. Prices do not include applicable taxes. Sales tax applicable in N.Y. Canadian residents will be charged applicable taxes. Offer not valid in Quebec. This offer is limited to one order per household. Not valid for current subscribers to Harlequin Presents books. All orders subject to credit approval. Credit or debit balances in a customer's account(s) may be offset by any other outstanding balance owed by or to the customer. Please allow 4 to 6 weeks for delivery. Offer available while quantities last.

Your Privacy—The Harlequin® Reader Service is committed to protecting your privacy. Our Privacy Policy is available online at www.ReaderService.com or upon request from the Harlequin Reader Service.

We make a portion of our mailing list available to reputable third parties that offer products we believe may interest you. If you prefer that we not exchange your name with third parties, or if you wish to clarify or modify your communication preferences, please visit us at www.ReaderService.com/consumerschoice or write to us at Harlequin Reader Service Preference Service, P.O. Box 9062, Buffalo, NY 14269. Include your complete name and address.

SPECIAL EXCERPT FROM

 **HARLEQUIN**®

Presents

Harlequin Presents welcomes you to the world of
THE CHATSFIELD; *synonymous with style,*
spectacle…and scandal!
Read on for an exclusive extract from Trish Morey's
contribution to this exciting eight-book series:
TYCOON'S TEMPTATION

* * *

SHE pointed, eager to distract him before he felt that crazy drumbeat, and held her breath as she felt the slide of his fingers under her ponytail, searching, probing her skull.

"This has to go," he said, sliding down her hair tie, the tug of it pulling at her hair and making her scalp tingle.

Her hair fell in a thick curtain around her face as his fingers returned, sliding under the weight of it, until her breathing grew shallow.

"Ow," she said, flinching a little as a fingertip grazed the site. "Just there."

"Let me see," he said, parting the hair around the spot, tilting her head in his hands so he could see in the dim light cast by the fringed light shade.

She didn't dare breathe. It was enough to feel. It was enough to trace the path of nerves connecting with nerves until she tingled from her head down to her toes and all the places in between. And she wondered about the touch of a man who could make her feel so much with just his fingers to her scalp—and how it would feel if he slid those fingers anywhere near the places where she really tingled—over the nub of her rock-hard nipples, or near the pulsing heat between her thighs.

"It's only a graze but you're going to have a bump," he said, and she stirred, his breath puffing at her hair. That sent a new wave of sensation rolling through her, pooling down low and hot in the pit of her belly. "You might want to ice that when you get back."

And suddenly his hands were gone and she swayed backward before she remembered.

Oh, yes. "Back" as in home, where she'd been in such a rush to get to a scant minute or two ago, before this man had laced his fingers through her hair and set her scalp alight and made her forget who he was.

A Chatsfield.

* * *

Step into the gilded world of **THE CHATSFIELD!**
Where secrets and scandal lurk behind every door…
Reserve your room!
September 2014.

HARLEQUIN® *Presents*®

Revenge and seduction intertwine…

Harlequin Presents welcomes you to the
world of The Chatsfield:
Synonymous with style, spectacle…and scandal!

SHEIKH'S SCANDAL by *Lucy Monroe* May 2014

PLAYBOY'S LESSON by *Melanie Milburne* June 2014

SOCIALITE'S GAMBLE by *Michelle Conder* July 2014

BILLIONAIRE'S SECRET by *Chantelle Shaw* August 2014

TYCOON'S TEMPTATION by *Trish Morey* September 2014

RIVAL'S CHALLENGE by *Abby Green* October 2014

REBEL'S BARGAIN by *Annie West* November 2014

HEIRESS'S DEFIANCE by *Lynn Raye Harris* December 2014

Step into the gilded world of The Chatsfield!
Where secrets and scandal lurk behind
every door…

Reserve your room!

www.Harlequin.com

HP132492